Acting Edition

I0591730

The Miss Magnolia Senior Citizen Beauty Pageant

by Leslie Kimbell

‖SAMUEL FRENCH‖

FOR PRODUCTION INQUIRIES

UNITED STATES AND CANADA
info@concordtheatricals.com
1-866-979-0447

UNITED KINGDOM AND EUROPE
licensing@concordtheatricals.co.uk
020-7054-7298

Each title is subject to availability from Concord Theatricals Corp.,
depending upon country of performance. Please be aware that THE
MISS MAGNOLIA SENIOR CITIZEN BEAUTY PAGEANT may not be
licensed by Concord Theatricals Corp. in your territory. Professional
and amateur producers should contact the nearest Concord Theatricals
Corp. office or licensing partner to verify availability.

MUSIC AND THIRD-PARTY MATERIALS USE NOTE

IMPORTANT BILLING AND CREDIT REQUIREMENTS

THE MISS MAGNOLIA SENIOR CITIZEN BEAUTY PAGEANT received its World Premiere Production at Winder Barrow Community Theatre in Winder, Georgia on October 8, 2021. It was directed by Léland Downs Karas and assistant director Kim Jones. The scenic design was by Leslie Kimbell and Léland Downs Karas. The lighting and sound were by Pamela Veader. Costume and Little Peanut design was by Eddie Nadeau. The cast was as follows:

BEATRICE SHELTON. . . . . Billie Nye-Muller

EADDY MAE CLAYTON . . . . Elinor Hasty

IMOGENE FLETCHER. . . . . .Candace Stoffel

MAUDE JENKINS . . . . .Ann Mitchell

SAM SMITH. . . . . Thomas Manley

LURLEEN DUPREE . . . . Andrea Fife

CLOVIS CROWN . . . . David Sullivan

MARTHA PARCELL . . . . Beverly Rutledge

HAZEL DILLARD . . . . .Lynn Mulvey

A NURSE . . . . Wendy Blessing-Toney

Voice-over work was provided by Carol Phillpotts and Scott Jones.

CHARACTERS

BEATRICE SHELTON – Sassy and salty senior citizen...retired Burlesque dancer.

EADDY MAE CLAYTON – Desperately religious Senior Citizen.

IMOGENE FLETCHER – Snarky senior citizen and wife to Sam.

MAUDE JENKINS – Dingy and pageant obsessed senior citizen.

SAM SMITH – Senior citizen. Reformed Casanova and husband to Imogene.

LURLEEN DUPREE – Thirties/fifties, Worn out and weary pageant coordinator.

CLOVIS CROWN – Awkward and nerdy senior citizen.

MARTHA PARCELL – A snooty senior citizen. The villain.

HAZEL DILLARD – Christmas obsessed and squirrel loving octogenarian.

SETTING

Magnolia Place Assisted Living Facility in Petula, Georgia
– Various locations.

TIME

Spring 1999.

AUTHOR'S NOTES

Imogene is: EYE-MO-JEAN

Eaddy is: Ee-dee

Beatrice is: Bee-uh-triss

The ladies' evening gowns and talent are written to give the actors, director and costume designer the freedom to be creative and have fun. However, the talent for each contestant should never be over two minutes thirty seconds.

These are real people and should not be portrayed as caricatures.

Lurleen's cell phone should be a 1990's flip phone.

It is not important that Imogene or Eaddy be good singers. A bad singer just adds to the fun.

The squirrel that attacks Hazel should be flat on her face...perhaps using a pair of glasses to have his arms clinging to the sides of the face. Have fun making this prop.

The inflatable date doll should be a fun and silly prop and not crude.

The pageant contestants should wear their number on a gold disc for gown and talent on the front of their costume. Martha's talent number should be on her back.

Orange hairspray works great for the "spray tanning incident."

It is my desire to create roles for senior actors, who are often overlooked for theatrical roles. However, the senior roles can be portrayed by any actor with the magic of theatrical makeup.

For Billie Nye-Muller
I too, would have taken my kitty to a different vet!

ACT I

Scene One

(Lights up stage left. In a pool of light **EADDY MAE CLAYTON** *stands in front of a door which serves as a backdrop and tries to adjust a sign displayed with the show title* "Senior Moments – Cable Access 14." *The sign slips and swings down on one corner to reveal a sign that reads "Janitor's Closet" underneath.* **EADDY** *gives up and leaves the sign hanging. There are two chairs on either side of a small table which holds a simple floral arrangement. A mop bucket, mop and broom sit beside the stage left chair.* **MARTHA PARCELL** *enters as* **EADDY** *shoves the mop bucket and broom out of the way. They sit. From the forced and sugar-coated way they speak to one another, we can tell that they do not like each other.* **EADDY** *reviews her cue cards.)*

EADDY. Martha...just as soon as the camera guy is ready... we'll get started.

MARTHA. It smells like bleach cleaner in here.

EADDY. Uh...huh...now did you have a chance to look over the questions I gave you?

MARTHA. Yes, and I rewrote all of them properly...you know...grammar...spelling...punctuation...

1

(MARTHA *gives* EADDY *a piece of paper.*
EADDY *balls up the paper and tosses it.*)

EADDY. Now honey...I don't want to get into your personal business...but remind me...how many times have you entered the Miss Magnolia Pageant? Fifteen...twenty?

MARTHA. *(Miffed.)* Three times. Just. Three.

EADDY. *(Sweetly.)* Well...I think it's so brave of you to enter, year after year...and *lose* again and again so gracefully. It must be difficult to always be first runner up...or as I call it...the first loser.

MARTHA. I *WAS* Miss Magnolia two years ago –

EADDY. Oh...no...no ma'am...*you* were the first runner up...and were only given the title after the real winner, Janette Simmons slipped and broke her hip in the jacuzzi room under *very* mysterious circumstances. I have it all right here on paper Martha.

(EADDY *gives an all-knowing look.*)

MARTHA. I hope you're not insinuating that I had anything to do with Janette's fall...and besides...*THAT* is just a technicality.

EADDY. Well...*technically*...that still means you lost. Anyway...I am just *thrilled* you could be on the show today.

MARTHA. Uh-huh...well... I am just so *thrilled* you asked me.

VOICE-OVER. OK everyone...please settle...and just watch for the red light...we're going *LIVE* in TEN.

MARTHA. *(Panic.)* Wait...LIVE...THIS IS LIVE!? I thought we were taping this.

EADDY. Oh no sugar...this is a live show. I must have forgotten to tell you...oh well...SMILE!

MARTHA. *(Extreme panic.)* OH, MY WORD! LIVE?

VOICE-OVER. We're live in Three...Two...One

> (*A peppy instrumental intro plays.** **MARTHA** *stares into the camera panicked.*)

Hey lady...we're live...you're on...you're on!!!

EADDY. Oh... Oh...sorry...yeah... Hey y'all and welcome to *Senior Moments* on your local Petula cable access Channel 14...coming to you LIVE from Magnolia Place Assisted Living and proudly sponsored by Judy's Beauty Shop and Small Engine Repair. I'm your host Eaddy Mae Clayton. Unfortunately, our original guest, Lurleen Dupree, could not be here today...and so...we're talking to Magnolia Place resident, Martha Parcell, about the upcoming Miss Magnolia Senior Citizen Pageant...and her *sad* and *desperate* attempt to win over the last four years. Now, Martha...tell the viewers...what do we have to look forward to this year?

> (**MARTHA** *is frozen.*)

Martha? (*Beat.*) Martha?

> (**EADDY** *smiles into the camera as she tries to nonchalantly poke* **MARTHA**.)

Martha honey...a little birdie told me you *might* be singing. (*Beat.*) Why don't you tell us what you'll be wearing?

MARTHA. (*Blankly.*) I'm uh...Martha...hello...what...who?

EADDY. (*Grasping.*) I uh...believe you were going to tell us something about this year's *Miss Magnolia Senior Citizen Beauty Pageant* sugar.

---

* A license to produce *The Miss Magnolia Senior Citizen Beauty Pageant* does not include a performance license for any third-party or copyrighted music. Licensees should create an original composition or use music in the public domain. For further information, please see the Music and Third-Party Materials Use Note on page iii.

MARTHA. *(Blankly.)* Hi...I'm Martha...uh...I...uh...I dance... I twirl... I dance –

EADDY. Uh-huh... *(Beat.)* Well...it sounds like we can count on something...just...*really* special.

> *(**MARTHA** is overcome with anxiety and reaches out toward the camera.)*

MARTHA. LIVE...LIVE TELEVISION! Ahhhhhhh –

> *(**MARTHA** faints. **EADDY** leaps to her feet and attempts to block **MARTHA** from the camera.)*

VOICE-OVER. DO SOMETHING! HEY LADY...GO TO COMMERCIAL!!

EADDY. What? OH...yes...well that sounds like it's going to be a pageant that no one will want to miss...doesn't it? So...um...we'll be back after this commercial from Judy's Beauty Shop and Small Engine Repair...for all your cutting, curling and lawn mower repair needs... Stay Tuned.

> *(Blackout.)*

Scene Two

(We are in the day room of Magnolia Place, an upscale assisted living home in Petula, Georgia. The room is decorated beautifully in a 1980's motif of country blue and mauve. A sofa and coffee table flanked by a pair of chairs is center. Stage right is an open arch leading to the resident's apartments. Upstage center is the double open archway leading to the medical offices and dining room. A sign with arrows indicates that the dining room is stage right and the offices are stage left. Downstage left is the breezeway to the convalescent wing of the facility. On either side of the upstage center archway are another set of matching wingback chairs and side tables with cloisonné lamps. Period appropriate artwork adorns the walls. There is a bulletin board on the stage right wall. A poster advertising the upcoming Miss Magnolia Senior Citizen Beauty Pageant is tacked on. There is a low bookcase containing games, puzzles, and books under the bulletin board.)

(There is a window stage left with curtains and sheers. There is a small console table downstage of the window. MAUDE, BEATRICE, and IMOGENE are seated on the sofa, center, gathered around the television watching the end of "Senior Moments"*...mouths agape. MAUDE wears a "MISS MAGNOLIA" sash and a rhinestone crown. IMOGENE is wearing an oxygen cannula connected to a rolling oxygen tank. We hear EADDY's voice coming from the television.)*

EADDY. "So...um...we'll be back after this commercial from Judy's Beauty Shop and Small Engine Repair...for all your cutting, curling and lawn mower repair needs... stay tuned."

> (**MAUDE** *turns off the television with a remote. There is stunned silence and then they all burst into laughter.*)

BEATRICE. *(Mocking.)* I'm uh...Martha... I'm Martha... I dance...uh uh...I twirl –

MAUDE. Bless her heart –

IMOGENE. Poor thing looked like a deer in headlights.

BEATRICE. I think this is the best episode...since Vera Mumford ate all those bourbon balls and flashed everyone during the Senior Gals on the Go Christmas Carol Sing-Along.

OH YEAH...that was great!

IMOGENE. Everyone in Petula saw her boobs.

MAUDE. I was sure they would cancel the show after that.

BEATRICE. And I'm sure that all four viewers would have been devastated.

> (*Enter* **EADDY MAE CLAYTON** *left. She has just come from the basement where she does the show.*)

EADDY. Hey y'all.

IMOGENE. Why didn't you go back on the air?

EADDY. I just told them to throw on an old episode. Are y'all talking about Vera's flashing incident again?

IMOGENE.	MAUDE.
Yes.	Uh-huh.

BEATRICE. Why is it that we always seem to be talkin' about tits?

EADDY. Beatrice...I have asked you on more than one occasion to call them... *(Whisper.) breasts.*

BEATRICE. TITS TITS TITS.

EADDY. RUDE!

BEATRICE. PRUDE!

EADDY. WITCH!

BEATRICE. BITCH!

IMOGENE. Y'all give me *serious* anxiety.

> *(**IMOGENE** cranks up her oxygen and takes a deep breath.)*

BEATRICE. Whatever

> *(**EADDY** suddenly begins to pray loudly.)*

EADDY. Dear Lord...please forgive me for my association with this pack of hell bound sinners. I know they are a blight on my otherwise saintly life. But I am weak Lord...and easily mislead down that rocky path...of sin...sin...sin. AMEN

BEATRICE. Thank you Miss Holy Roller 1998!

EADDY. Thank *you*...Mary Magdalene.

> *(**MAUDE** rises and crosses to the bulletin board and points at the Miss Magnolia Pageant poster.)*

MAUDE. Would you look at this? I cannot believe Lurleen didn't put my name or my picture on this poster. After all, I *am* the current reigning Miss Magnolia.

IMOGENE. They don't need to Maude...you never take off the crown.

MAUDE. I take if off when I get in the shower...*sometimes.*

EADDY. You probably sleep in it.

MAUDE. *(Defensive.)* Not *every* night.

BEATRICE. Maude Jenkins...you are ridiculous and –

MAUDE. Don't be jealous Beatrice. We can't all be queen... someone has to clap as I walk by.

BEATRICE. Will somebody hit that button?

IMOGENE. What button?

BEATRICE. You know...the button you press that makes the floor open...and then she falls into a big hole.

EADDY. Even *I* would press that button. *(Then.)* Forgive me Lord.

BEATRICE. I think *anyone* who needs to enter a beauty pageant for attention...is just pitiful and needy.

IMOGENE. Says the former *burlesque queen* of New York.

BEATRICE. *Excuse me*...I was not looking for attention... I was an *entertainer*...it was my job. You wouldn't catch me *dead* in an old lady beauty pageant.

EADDY. I don't want to get into your personal business... but I hardly think that swinging tassels on your breasts, qualifies you as an *(Air quotes.) entertainer*, Beatrice.

IMOGENE. Oh, now I think that would be *real* entertaining.

MAUDE. I agree...glamorous and exciting. Remind me... what was your stripper name Beatrice?

BEATRICE. *(Striking a sexy pose.)* Miss Bang Bang LaDish...The Best Guns in the West.

EADDY. She could do a striptease, twirl a lasso, and swing both of her bullet pasties in two different directions... all at the same time.

IMOGENE. How on earth did you learn to twirl things with your boobs?

BEATRICE.   I went to the Pink Pussycat College of Striptease. *(Then.)* But...I taught *myself* how to twirl my tassels...because the tassel twirling professor they had was terrible.

EADDY. Tassel twirling *professor*?

MAUDE. You taught yourself?

BEATRICE. Yeah...sure...it's easy really...just watch this –

EADDY. OH NO Beatrice...not again –

IMOGENE. You're gonna do it now?

EADDY. This will not end well...you may as well go ahead and call 911 now.

> (**BEATRICE** *moves center and the others surround her. She begins to shimmy her right shoulder back and forth...rocking forward and back, thrusting her bosom up and down.*)

BEATRICE. You just have to know how to work your shoulders to get your tassels twirling. *(Beat.)* Now...just pretend I'm topless.

> (**EADDY** *covers her eyes and moans.*)

EADDY. Noooo –

MAUDE. What's wrong?

EADDY. I've seen this before...it's not pretty. *(Then.)* You might want to rethink this Beatrice...you know what happened last time.

BEATRICE. OK...now...once ya get the right one going good...you get started on the left one.

> (**BEATRICE** *begins to alternate shoulder movements.*)

EADDY. She tried showing me this once...and ended up in the emergency room with a slipped disc and two black eyes.

IMOGENE. *(To* **EADDY.***)* Black eyes?

EADDY. She was *actually* topless –

> *(***EADDY** *mimics two sagging boobs flying up and hitting her in the face.)*

Boom Boom...get it?

BEATRICE. OK...now here comes the left –

> *(***BEATRICE** *continues to shimmy her right shoulder and then alternates with her left shoulder.)*

It's easy...c'mon...y'all try it. Just close your eyes...and pretend you've got some tassels on your tits. *(She looks at* **EADDY.***)* Sorry...*Breasts.*

> *(***IMOGENE** *and* **MAUDE** *close their eyes and begin to grunt and strain as they shimmy and roll their shoulders awkwardly.* **MAUDE** *is particularly animated as she prances about holding her bosoms.* **EADDY** *watches them, frowning.)*

IMOGENE. Is it supposed to hurt like this?

BEATRICE. *(Grunting.)* Not once you get the hang of it.

MAUDE. *(Getting excited.)* OH YEAH...SHAKE IT... WORK IT...HOW YA LIKE ME NOW BOYS? WOO HOO!

IMOGENE. I can't believe I'm doing this... I feel like something is gonna fall off.

EADDY. I think we need to pray. Dear Lord...please forgive my terrible and sinful lack of judgement with the people I associate with. I am so ashamed of my –

(Unnoticed, **SAM SMITH** *and* **CLOVIS CROWN** *enter stage right.* **SAM** *wears a polyester leisure suit, loud shirt, gold chains and white patent loafers.* **CLOVIS** *is the nerd type with high waisted pants and, mismatched shirt, dark socks, and thick eyeglasses. He has a slight limp. He is stunned, mouth open and head spinning.)*

SAM. HUBBA HUBBA...

(The ladies scream.)

I would ask you what's shakin'... but I can see.

IMOGENE. Sam Smith...you scared the daylights out of us!

*(***CLOVIS***'s head continues to spin.* **BEATRICE** *snaps her fingers in his face...his mouth still agape.)*

BEATRICE. Who's this idiot?

SAM. Ladies...I would like to introduce you to my new friend Clovis Crown. He just moved in today.

CLOVIS. *(Awkward.)* Good afternoon ladies.

*(***SAM*** *crosses to* **IMOGENE** *and pulls her in for a kiss and a smack on the bottom.)*

SAM. Hey there sexy mama...did you miss me?

IMOGENE. You know I did daddy.

SAM. Clovis...this is my sexy wife Imogene.

CLOVIS. Nice to meet you Imogene.

SAM. Ain't she foxy?

CLOVIS. *(Timid.)* Oh yes...very...um...foxy.

*(***SAM*** *turns to* **CLOVIS** *and whispers.)*

SAM. Stand there like a stud and I'll get you a date.

(**CLOVIS** *steps forward and makes a comically awkward attempt to strike a studly pose.*)

SAM. Uh...so ladies...Clovis here is single and ready to mingle. Who wants to be the first lucky lady to show him around town?

(**CLOVIS** *adjusts his glasses and smiles.* **MAUDE, BEATRICE** *and* **EADDY** *look nervously at each other.*)

MAUDE. Um... I'm sorry...but I'm pretty sure I have an appointment to wash my hair today.

EADDY. *(Looks at watch.)* Oh...would you look at that... I'm late for my prayer meeting.

BEATRICE. *(Dry.)* I'd rather eat dirt.

(**CLOVIS** *is crestfallen.*)

CLOVIS. Well...I guess I'll be going... I've got things to unpack and so forth and so on and what have you... nice meeting you ladies. I'm sure I'll see you around sometime.

(**CLOVIS** *exits right.*)

BEATRICE. What a geek.

SAM. That was awful mean of you ladies. Why couldn't one of you take him out and show him the town?

BEATRICE. Excuse me? I can't be seen in public with an old nerd like that. I have a reputation to protect.

SAM. It's more likely that we need to protect everyone from *your* reputation.

BEATRICE. Imogene...are you gonna let your husband talk to me like that?

IMOGENE. If the shoe fits darlin' –

EADDY. Amen sister!

MAUDE. You *are* a slut Beatrice.

BEATRICE. I'm not saying I hate y'all...but don't leave me in charge of your life support –

SAM. OK...well I'm gonna go check on Clovis... I'm sure y'all hurt his feelings.

IMOGENE. Wait sugar britches...you look hungry...let me give you a snack. It's some of those yummy cheese crackers you like.

> (**IMOGENE** *reaches into her purse and gives* **SAM** *a pack of crackers.*)

SAM. Thanks...I'll see you later...sweet cheeks.

> (**SAM** *turns to* **IMOGENE** *to give her a kiss and a swat on the bottom.* **IMOGENE** *giggles and waves as* **SAM** *points his finger and makes the chick-chick sound, then exits.*)

IMOGENE. I'll miss you big daddy! *(Then firmly.)* Let that be a lesson ladies. *Never* let your man leave horny or hungry...because somewhere out there...is a whore with a sandwich...just waiting to swoop in.

> (*Enter* **HAZEL DILLARD,** *a wacky woman in her eighties. She is decked out in Christmas attire. She uses a rolling walker with a seat which holds a small cage for her pet squirrel, Little Peanut.*)

HAZEL. Merry Christmas y'all...what's going on?

IMOGENE. *(Sigh and eye roll.)* Hazel honey...it's not Christmas.

HAZEL. Y'all know I celebrate Christmas...all year long. Who wants to come Christmas caroling with me and Little Peanut?

EADDY. It's *April* honey...aren't you tired of people throwing eggs at you?

BEATRICE. I cannot believe you walk around Magnolia Place dressed like a demented elf, carrying that rodent in a cage. They're gonna come lock you up in the looney bin.

HAZEL. Little Peanut is *NOT* a rodent! He's *family* –

MAUDE. *(Squinting into the cage.)* Is that squirrel wearing a tutu?

HAZEL. *(Gushing.)* Yeah...isn't he adorable... I made it myself...and wait until you see the little Santa suit I'm knitting him...it gonna say...Hazel's Little Peanut, on the front. *(She giggles.)*

BEATRICE. It should say Miss Hazel *IS* a nut!

HAZEL. I see Beatrice is in one of her moods today. I'll see y'all later...but remind me to tell you about my talent for the Miss Magnolia Pageant.

MAUDE. Oh...*you're* entering the pageant?

HAZEL. Yes...Little Peanut and I have been working on a very special talent presentation.

IMOGENE. What is it?

HAZEL. Well...I was going to let it be a surprise...but...if y'all promise you won't tell –

MAUDE.	**EADDY.**	**IMOGENE.**
We wouldn't dream of it.	Of course, not.	Mum's the word.

BEATRICE. *(Mumble.)* Who gives a crap?

HAZEL. *(Excited.)* We're gonna be doing a little duet... I'm gonna sing "Jingle Bells"...and Little Peanut is gonna play his tambourine. Look...isn't it cute –

> (**HAZEL** *pulls out a tiny squirrel sized tambourine. Everyone leans in, squinting to see it.*)

EADDY. Where on earth did you get such a teensy little tambourine like that.

HAZEL. *(Pleased.)* I made it myself from a Coca-Cola cap. Isn't it cute?

BEATRICE. *(Sarcastic.)* How innovative of you.

IMOGENE. You *actually* taught a squirrel to play the tambourine?

HAZEL. Oh yeah...Little Peanut just sets up on top of my head...and shakes it and shakes it...of course I have to duct tape it to his little hand...but he loves it. *(Then.)* Well, I gotta get going.

> *(**HAZEL** turns stage right and exits singing "Jingle Bells.")*

BEATRICE. *(Calling after her.)* Yeah...I'm calling the ASPCA...ANIMAL ABUSER!

EADDY. Be nice Beatrice...you know she's crazy as a loon.

> *(There is a crash off stage, and we hear a voice.)*

LURLEEN. *(Offstage.)* DAMMIT! WHO LEFT A WHEELCHAIR IN THE MIDDLE OF THE FLOOR? Why does everything have to be so dammed difficult? Why do I let myself get roped into this pageant crap year after year after year?

> *(A fabulously dressed **LURLEEN DUPREE**, fifties, enters backwards stage right pulling a small rolling garment rack full of dresses, gowns, boas, and colorful costumes. A shelf on top holds a couple of wigs on wig heads and hats. She struggles to carry a tote bag, easel and poster advertising The Bell of The Ball Evening Wear Emporium. **MAUDE** rushes to the rack and starts pawing at everything with glee.)*

MAUDE. OOOOOOOO SHINY!!!!!!

LURLEEN. *(Taken aback.)* Oh goodness...hey ladies...I didn't expect y'all to be in here.

BEATRICE. Obviously –

MAUDE. Sequins!

IMOGENE. It looks like you brought the whole store with you.

> *(**LURLEEN** pops open the easel and puts the poster on it.)*

LURLEEN. Oh, honey no...this is nothing –

MAUDE. *(Mesmerized.)* Everything is so shiny! I love shiny! OOOO shiny!

> *(**MAUDE** disappears behind the rolling rack.)*

LURLEEN. I'm sorry I'm so crabby y'all... I'm just a little stressed out... My van wouldn't start and then I broke a nail...and *then* Gaynelle quit down at the store... anyway...let's get this show on the road...the sooner we do it...the sooner it's over. So, who all's entering the pageant?

> *(**LURLEEN** pulls a clipboard out of her tote and looks at her list.)*

EADDY.	IMOGENE.	BEATRICE.
I'm not.	Don't look at me.	Oh hell no.

LURLEEN. So...wait...that means I only have *(She checks her list.)* one...two...*TWO* contestants? Hazel Dillard and Martha Parcell? We may as well not do it...I mean...I need at least four contestants.

> *(**LURLEEN** is thrilled with the news that she won't have to do the pageant after all...but feigns sadness.)*

Well...I guess that means no pageant this year...too bad...so sad...I guess I need to load up all this crap and take it on back down to the store.

(**MAUDE** *pops out from behind the rolling rack wearing a flashy sequin jacket and feather boa.*)

MAUDE.
HERE SHE IS...MISS MAGNOLIA SENIOR CITIZEN. LOOK AT ME –

BEATRICE. *(Firmly.)* NO!

MAUDE. *(Softly.)* ...don't I look fiiiiine?

LURLEEN. Please don't play with the sequins Ms. Jenkins.

MAUDE. So, do I get to be Miss Magnolia for another whole year then?

LURLEEN. Yes...I guess so Ms. Jenkins...good for you! Well...alright...bye then –

(**LURLEEN** *tries to exit.*)

BEATRICE. Wait...wait wait wait...so are you saying we will have to deal with Maude traipsing around Magnolia Place waving her hand like the Queen of England in that crown and sash for another year?

LURLEEN. Looks that way –

BEATRICE. *(Not having it.)* Excuse us for just a second please.

(**BEATRICE** *pulls* **IMOGENE** *and* **EADDY** *down left into a huddle.*)

LURLEEN. *(Confused.)* Um...o-kayy –

BEATRICE. Listen to me... I am not going to put up with another year of Maude's madness...so y'all are doing the pageant. Got it?

IMOGENE.	EADDY.
Excuse me?	I don't think so.

BEATRICE. Oh yes you are...so strap your extra turbo strength girdles on those big ole' butts and get ready –

IMOGENE. Why don't you haul your saggy butt up there and swing your tassels or something?

EADDY. Oh honey...*nobody* wants to see that.

IMOGENE. Well Beatrice?

BEATRICE. *(Suddenly frail.)* I can't...you know I have a bad back...and the arthur-I-tis –

EADDY.	IMOGENE.
What?	Since when?

(**BEATRICE** *holds her back as if in pain.*)

EADDY. Well...the "*arthur-I-tis*" hasn't stopped you from throwin' your legs up in the air for every Tom, Dick and Harry at Magnolia Place...and the rest of the tri-state area.

BEATRICE. Thank you Sister Mary Holier Than Thou Supreme.

EADDY. You're welcome...Maria Von Trashy.

(**BEATRICE** *crosses to* **LURLEEN.**)

BEATRICE. OK...these two heifers are gonna do it...so now you have enough contestants.

LURLEEN. Oh...great! I was so disappointed.

(*We hear* **MARTHA PARCELL** *screaming off stage.*)

MARTHA. *(Offstage.)* EADDY MAE CLAYTON!!!

LURLEEN. What in the world?

EADDY. Oh Lord...the gates of hell have opened, and she has emerged.

IMOGENE. Who is that?

BEATRICE. It's Martha Parcell...and she's on the war path.

LURLEEN. She sounds like she's ready to kill somebody –

EADDY. Yeah...it's me.

IMOGENE. Well then...hide Eaddy... HIDE!

>*(**MAUDE** comes out from behind the rolling rack and drags **EADDY** behind the rack.)*

MAUDE. Don't worry...I got this.

>*(**EADDY** disappears behind the rolling rack with **MAUDE** as **MARTHA** storms in.)*

MARTHA. Where's Eaddy?

IMOGENE.	**LURLEEN.**
Who?	Eaddy?

MARTHA. Don't even try it...where is she??

>*(The clothing rack begins to roll stage right. **MAUDE** and **EADDY** giggle.)*

Who's back there?

>*(**MAUDE** steps out from behind the rolling rack.)*

MAUDE. It's just me...Maude Jenkins...and...my...uh... cousin...from...Euro...pia...*Euro-pia.*

MARTHA. Euro-pia?

>*(**EADDY** steps out wearing a big hat, sunglasses, and a boa. She speaks in a bad, mish mosh accent.)*

EADDY. Pore-fay-vore. Par-lay voo frenchy?... It is a moo-cho pleasure-eeto to meet you madame-wah-zell. Wiener schnitzel.

> (**EADDY** *inches toward the stage right doorway.*)

MARTHA. *(Leery.)* Yes...it's nice to meet you too.

EADDY. Well... Frère Jacques, Frère Jacques ding dang dong...and hasta lay vista...y'all.

MAUDE. Yes...uh...she is saying that we have to go now... adios, chow and pasta lay way-go.

> (**MARTHA** *stares suspiciously after* **MAUDE** *and* **EADDY** *as they rapidly exit.*)

MARTHA. *(Suspicious.)* Wait a minute –

LURLEEN. *(Interrupting.)* So...I'll see you tomorrow at pageant rehearsal Ms. Parcell?

MARTHA. *(Full attention.)* Oh yes...of course. So, who all do you have in the pageant so far? Or should I say...who will be the losers?

> (**LURLEEN** *looks at her clipboard.*)

LURLEEN. Well...we have *you*...Hazel Dillard...Imogene Smith...and Eaddy Mae Clayton.

MARTHA. EADDY IS IN THE PAGEANT?

LURLEEN. Yes...she just decided today.

BEATRICE. Why do you ask Martha? Are you afraid you might lose...again?

MARTHA. AFRAID? Of course, not...everyone knows this is my year. Besides...I didn't hear your name on that list.

BEATRICE. I don't do pageants Martha...they're for sad and desperate people with low self-esteem.

(**MARTHA** *gets up in* **BEATRICE**'s *face.*)

MARTHA. Desperate?

BEATRICE. You heard me.

MARTHA. Beatrice Shelton don't test my sweet southern belle charm darlin'. Maybe it's *you* who's scared.

BEATRICE. Scared? I'm not *scared*!

MARTHA. Well then...I dare you!

BEATRICE. Dare me to what?

MARTHA. I *dare you* to enter the pageant!

(**MARTHA** *and* **BEATRICE** *get in each other's face.*)

BEATRICE. OK WITCHYPOO, YOU'RE ON!!!

MARTHA. GREAT! See ya there Broom Hilda!

(**MARTHA** *struts off stage left cackling.* **MAUDE** *and* **EADDY** *poke their heads in the door.*)

MAUDE. Is the coast clear?

IMOGENE. Yes –

LURLEEN. Lord give me strength...y'all are gonna give me a nervous breakdown. *(Beat.)* OK...with Ms. Shelton... that makes five contestant total.

BEATRICE. *(Confused.)* Wait...what just happened?

IMOGENE. Looks like you're in the pageant darlin'.

EADDY. Hope you have an extra turbo strength girdle for that big ole' butt Beatrice.

BEATRICE. Well SHIT!

(Blackout.)

Scene Three

(A few minutes later. Down Left – Pool of light. A sign reads "Jacuzzi Room." There is a handwritten paper taped to the sign that reads "Jacuzzi Room Permanently Closed." Clovis attempts to make studly poses. Enter **SAM SMITH** *eating his snack.)*

SAM. There you are...I've been looking all over for you Clovis...what are you doing...are you okay?

CLOVIS. Oh man...I'm such a doofus.

SAM. Hey now...don't get discouraged man... I got your back...don't worry.

CLOVIS. Forget it Sam...I'm just a big ole' nerd and all those ladies know it.

SAM. You're not a nerd Clovis. We just need to work on a few things...like your mannerisms...and your walk...and your clothes...and...well...pretty much...everything.

CLOVIS. You mean you'll help me with the ladies?

SAM. Absolutely man...that's what friends are for.

CLOVIS. Thanks Sam...I guess you've been with a lot of ladies...you're so...suave and debonair.

SAM. *(Cocky.)* Oh yeah...sure sure...lots of ladies. Back in the day man...when I was working in Vegas as an Elvis Impersonator...the ladies loved me...they would clap and scream and throw their motel room keys and panties at me on the stage.

CLOVIS. *(Scowls.)* They threw their panties?

SAM. Oh yeah –

CLOVIS. Well...that just seems unsanitary.

*(**SAM** is dumbfounded.)*

SAM. Uh yeah...anyway...all it takes is the right attitude... and the right clothes...and we'll have a hot dame on your arm in no time.

CLOVIS. *(Excited.)* OK...what do we do first?

SAM. Well...let's start with the walk. *(Beat.)* I noticed you just kinda' shuffle like an old man. Here now...show me how you walk.

> (**CLOVIS** *shuffles a few steps awkwardly with a bit of a limp.*)

CLOVIS. How's that? I know I limp a little...I have ingrown toenails.

SAM. OK...that's not good...you need to have a cockier walk. You can't be doing all the limping...makes you look old and decrepit. Let me show you.

> (**SAM** *demonstrates a very studly walk... smiling, pointing, and flirting with "all the ladies.")*

CLOVIS. Oh wow...I don't think I'm ready for that level of studly-ness. Maybe we better start somewhere else...a little easier.

SAM. No way...your walk is your calling card...it's your ticket to getting the ladies attention. Now...stand up straight and hold your head up. Strut like me...like a *stud. (Beat.)* OK now...show me what a big stud you are...show me how to walk in the room and command attention.

> (**CLOVIS** *attempts to mimic* **SAM***'s walk and attitude. He is pitiful...ending in an awkward pose.*)

SAM. Yeah...OK maybe we better start somewhere else.

CLOVIS. *(Dejected.)* I'm never gonna get a girlfriend.

SAM. Don't say that Clovis...you can do it.

CLOVIS. I'm not so sure.

SAM. Well now...how did you meet ladies in the past?

CLOVIS. I didn't.

SAM. What do you mean?

CLOVIS. Just what I said...I didn't meet any ladies in the past.

SAM. You've *never* had a girlfriend?

CLOVIS. Nope...not even a date.

SAM. So you've never...uh...you know...

CLOVIS. Nope...never. I mean...one time a bunch of my friends felt sorry for me and hired me a *(Whisper.)* "lady of the evening." *(Then.)* But when she took off her top... I got so nervous that I threw up on her shoes. So...that didn't really work out.

SAM. Oh man...this is worse than I thought.

CLOVIS. Do you think I'm hopeless?

> (**SAM** *considers the question and then straightens up boldly.*)

SAM. NO WAY! You are not hopeless...not with Sam Smith on your side...besides...my reputation as the Magnolia Place Casanova is at stake here. *(Beat.)* Now...show me that walk again...and this time...hold that head up –

> (**CLOVIS** *stands up straight and begins to demonstrate the walk.*)

> *(Blackout.)*

Scene Four

(Lights up. The next day. We are back in the day room of Magnolia Place. An upbeat, 1980's Latin conga pop song plays.* A very animated **LURLEEN** *is attempting to teach a dance routine. She is graceful and elegant as she dances across the stage demonstrating the routine.* **MARTHA, HAZEL, EADDY, IMOGENE** *and* **BEATRICE** *are lined up across downstage attempting to follow the routine. They are exhausted and confused.* **IMOGENE** *is tangled in her oxygen hose.* **EADDY** *is off the beat.* **BEATRICE** *scowls and holds her boobs as if they hurt.* **HAZEL** *looks at the others and pushes her walker back and forth, bobbing her head.* **MARTHA** *prances about with confidence. The ladies all yell over the music.)*

LURLEEN. OK ladies...five six seven eight...feel the beat... and shake those maracas...shake 'em...shake 'em... I know you can do it. Shake that booty too...feel the heat...shake what your mama gave ya!

EADDY. *My* mama just rolled over in her grave!

*(**HAZEL** grabs at her back.)*

HAZEL. Oh my...my sciatica.

BEATRICE. I HATE YOU LURLEEN!

IMOGENE. DITTO!

EADDY. I THINK WE NEED TO PRAY!

---

* A license to produce *The Miss Magnolia Senior Citizen Beauty Pageant* does not include a performance license for any third-party or copyrighted music. Licensees should create an original composition or use music in the public domain. For further information, please see the Music and Third-Party Materials Use Note on page iii.

MARTHA. WOO HOO… LOOK AT ME …I'M FABULOUS!

IMOGENE. CAN SOMEBODY HELP ME? MY HOSE IS ALL KINKED UP!

> (**EADDY** *stops to help* **IMOGENE**. **MARTHA** *purposely bumps into* **EADDY** *causing her to fly across the stage dragging* **IMOGENE** *and her oxygen tank with her.*)

MARTHA. LET'S CONGA Y'ALL!!!

> (**LURLEEN** *stares with her mouth open. The ladies are now completely lost and just making anything up.*)

LURLEEN. Okay…Okay…OKAYYY stop…STOOOOPPP!

> (**LURLEEN** *turns off the music and all the ladies collapse on the sofa and chairs.*)

(Dry.) OK…so um…I think we'll just…uh…cancel the opening number.

EADDY. Thank you Lord!

BEATRICE. I'll second that.

> *(The ladies all move to sit down.)*

LURLEEN. Don't get too comfortable…we still need to work on our walking and smiles and waves.

> (**LURLEEN** *picks up a clipboard and checks it.*)

And…I'll need each of you to you get with me by the end of the day with your final decisions on your talent performance. So far…I've got Hazel and Little Peanut… doing "Jingle Bells"…and Martha Parcell –

MARTHA. I'm twirling my fire batons to "Disco Inferno" of course

IMOGENE. SHUT UP...REALLY? Now that I want to see.

EADDY. Dear Lord...please forgive me for the vile thoughts that just went through my head. I do not want Martha to set herself on fire –

MARTHA. WHA–

LURLEEN. Oh yes Ms. Parcell...about that...I talked to the fire marshal, and he would not sign off on it. Sorry...no fire batons.

MARTHA. WHAT??? But I've been practicing for weeks.

HAZEL. And set off the fire alarm...*twice*. It just about scared Little Peanut half to death.

LURLEEN. Uh huh...anyway...Ms. Clayton...what will you be doing?

EADDY. Well...not a lot of people know this...but I can throw my voice.

LURLEEN. *(Puzzled.)* What is that now?

EADDY. I'm a ventriloquist.

BEATRICE. Since when?

EADDY. Oh...since I was a kid...I used to do it at church and Bible school... I won the Little Miss Southern Baptist Darling Diva contest in 1939.

IMOGENE. How long has it been since you...uh... ventriloquist-ed –

EADDY. Oh, I don't know...ten...fifteen...sixty years... something like that. But it's like riding a bicycle...you never forget.

MARTHA. This oughta be good.

LURLEEN. And let's see...Ms. Smith...what will you be doing?

IMOGENE. I don't know... I don't have any talent really... maybe I can tell some jokes.

LURLEEN. OK...maybe jokes...not at all helpful, but thanks...and then that brings me to Ms. Shelton –

> *(Enter* **MAUDE JENKINS** *wearing her crown and sash...carrying a pair of tap shoes.)*

MAUDE. Sorry to interrupt girls...Lurleen...I...uh...couldn't help overhearing that you're cancelling the opening number...and I just wanted you to know that I can do my tap routine at the pageant if you'd like me to.

BEATRICE. Are you talking about when you clomp and stomp around like a herd of cattle?

LURLEEN. I might just take you up on that offer Ms. Jenkins... I'll let you know.

MAUDE. What are y'all doing in here...are you practicing your pageant wave? I can show you... I've got it down pat.

> *(***MAUDE*** *proceeds to grandly wave and smile as she crosses left and right.)*

LURLEEN. *(Forced.)* That's very good Ms. Jenkins.

MAUDE. Yes...I know –

LURLEEN. OK...why don't we all give it a try? Everyone line up there beside Ms. Jenkins...while I find my Valium.

> *(***LURLEEN*** *digs in her bag.* **MAUDE** *struts forward grandly waving. Not to be outdone,* **MARTHA** *struts forward beside her. Everyone else begrudgingly staggers forward into a line.)*

Let's go...come on...chop chop...you too Ms. Shelton... nothing wrong with practicing. OK?

BEATRICE. Practicing what?

LURLEEN. We are going to learn the Beauty Queen Elbow Elbow...Wrist Wrist...Step Pivot Turn.

IMOGENE. The what?

> (**LURLEEN** *quickly demonstrates.*)

MAUDE. *(Clapping.)* Oooo this is my favorite!

MARTHA. Me too!

BEATRICE. Elbow wrist what?

LURLEEN. *(Dreamy.)* It's the key to your whole pageant walk...handed down over the years by all the beauty pageant queens who came before you.

MAUDE. *(Gushing.)* Like me.

> (**LURLEEN** *begins to model and wave, moving her elbow side to side and swirling her wrist. The ladies follow suit...each in a different way. Only* **MARTHA** *and* **MAUDE** *take it seriously.*)

LURLEEN. Now...elbows high...above your heart...and... ready...elbow elbow...wrist wrist...big smiles...elbow elbow...wrist wrist...elbow elbow...wrist wrist...ooo... don't you feel beautiful? –

> (*An exasperated* **BEATRICE**, *stops and stares at everyone.*)

BEATRICE. Are you kidding me with this shit?

EADDY. I kinda like it... I feel pretty.

BEATRICE. Well, you look stupid...you *all* look stupid

LURLEEN. *AND*...now let's try it with some music...and –

(**LURLEEN** *turns on the CD player. Elegant and dreamy pageant walk music plays.**)

LURLEEN. Lovely...and elbow elbow...wrist wrist...and get ready for the turn...aaannd...watch closely...and...step forward...pivot...turn...again...step forward...pivot... turn... SMILE LADIES –

(**LURLEEN** *does a graceful step. pivot, turn. The ladies follow suit...and except for* **MARTHA** *and* **MAUDE** *...they each turn in different directions, tripping and bumping into each other.*)

HAZEL. Wait...is it left or right?

IMOGENE. Am I *supposed* to feel like I'm going to pass out Lurleen?

EADDY. What's happening? I'm so confused.

(**LURLEEN** *scowls but continues her graceful modeling.*)

LURLEEN. Step forward left...pivot turn right...and back forward...elbow elbow...wrist wrist –

(**MAUDE** *twirls forward and continues waving as she exits.*)

MAUDE. OK...keep up the good job ladies...maybe one day you'll be as fabulous as me...tah tah –

(**LURLEEN** *turns off the music as* **MAUDE** *exits.* **LURLEEN** *begins to gather her bag and CD player.*)

---

* A license to produce *The Miss Magnolia Senior Citizen Beauty Pageant* does not include a performance license for any third-party or copyrighted music. Licensees should create an original composition or use music in the public domain. For further information, please see the Music and Third-Party Materials Use Note on page iii. .

LURLEEN. OK...OK...so...now we have the basics of the... elbow elbow...wrist wrist...step pivot turn, down...you can all practice on your own.

MARTHA. Yes...*some* of us need *a lot* of practice.

> (**MARTHA** *crosses to the stage left doorway and turns back.*)

Not me of course...this is my year.

> (**MARTHA** *exits.*)

LURLEEN. I'll see you ladies tomorrow for the pageant.

> (**LURLEEN** *exits as a voice crackles over the intercom.*)

VOICE-OVER. Attention residents...could Hazel Dillard come to the infirmary please? Hazel Dillard to the infirmary please. Thank you.

HAZEL. Oh...that's me...I forgot about my appointment. *(Beat.)* Hey Eaddy...can you please watch Little Peanut for me this afternoon? I've gotta go for this check-up and get some squirrel food.

EADDY. Well, I –

HAZEL. Thank you so much Eaddy...you're a doll.

> (**HAZEL** *grabs the cage and thrusts it into* **EADDY**'s *hands.*)

EADDY. Hazel...I don't think –

HAZEL. He's asleep under his little blanket...he probably just needs a little water...but that's all...okay...see ya in a bit.

> (**HAZEL** *exits singing* "Deck The Halls."

BEATRICE. OK...what the hell? You're a squirrel sitter now?

EADDY. Don't start Beatrice...you know she's nuttier than a five-pound fruitcake.

(**BEATRICE** *grabs the cage and plops it on the coffee table.*)

CAREFUL BEATTY –

IMOGENE. OK girls... I'm off to Judy's for my wash-n-set... gotta keep sexy for my hunka hunka burnin' love.

BEATRICE. I have an appointment too...can I ride with you?

IMOGENE. Sure...I just need to grab my purse.

EADDY. Y'all have fun...I need to go soak in a tub of Bengay.

(**EADDY, IMOGENE** *and* **BEATRICE** *exit upstage center.*)

(*A beat later,* **MARTHA** *peers around the downstage left doorway, then creeps in and grabs Little Peanut's cage. She opens the cage, shakes it and sits it on the table by the window...then opens the window.*)

MARTHA. Let's see what little miss snooty britches thinks of this. *(Beat.)* Two birds with one stone... I'm sure to win now.

(**MARTHA** *exits left cackling.*)

(*Blackout.*)

Scene Five

(Thirty minutes later. SAM *sits on a park bench in the Magnolia Place courtyard.* CLOVIS *is still trying to work out his sexy walk.* SAM *calls out to someone in the distance.)*

SAM. Hey there Doris...lookin' good baby...lookin' *real* good!

*(*SAM *strikes a sexy pose and winks...shooting his "gun finger" and making the chick-chick sound.)*

CLOVIS. You make it look so easy.

SAM. What?

CLOVIS. Flirting with the ladies.

SAM. Well...I *am* a professional ya know.

CLOVIS. Yeah...so how am I doing with my sexy strut?

SAM. OK...show me again.

*(*CLOVIS *demonstrates his sexy and confident walk. It's better...but not quite there yet.)*

OK...OK...good job...it's gettin' there...I can see it...just keep practicing. Did you get a chance to work on any of those pick-up lines I wrote down for you?

CLOVIS. Oh yeah...I did...I was up all night –

*(*CLOVIS *pulls out a small notepad.)*

SAM. Great...let's hear them.

*(*CLOVIS *is awkward and stiff as he tries to read out the pick-up lines.)*

CLOVIS. OK...uh...Hey baby...are you...uh...cheese...um... on the floor?

> (**CLOVIS** *attempts to mimic* **SAM***'s gun and chick chick sound but fails miserably.*)

SAM. *(Confused.) What?* Give me that.

> (**SAM** *takes the notepad.*)

No...no...Clovis...you got two mixed up. Look here... it's... "Hey baby...are you cheese? Cause you look real *gouda*."

CLOVIS. Oh...yeah...right...right.

SAM. And the other one is...I love your dress...it would look *really good* on my floor.

CLOVIS. *(Dejected.)* Oh man...I'm never gonna get this right.

SAM. Here...let me show you how it's done. *(Beat.)* OK... so...you've got a sexy dame standing here...and so you –

> (**CLOVIS** *takes back the pad and pulls out a pen to take notes.*)

...give her a smile...and a little wink...and then you say... Hey baby...did it hurt? *(Beat.)* Then she says *(Feminine voice.)* Did what hurt? *(Beat.)* Then *you* say...When you fell out of heaven...because you *must* be an angel.

CLOVIS. *(Furiously writing.)* Oh...that's good...that's *real* good.

SAM. Now you try it.

CLOVIS. Uh huh...uh huh...OK...so I...give her a smile *(Big cheesy smile.)* and a wink *(More of a blink.)*...and then I say *(Sexy voice.)* Hey baby...did you...uh...get hurt when you fell over...fell down...on the cheese? Wait... no...that's not it –

(SAM's mouth falls open and then his head drops into his hand. CLOVIS looks at him with defeat.)

SAM. Uh...yeah...that was a good effort...but we've gotta keep working on it.

CLOVIS. I wouldn't blame you if you gave up on me... I'm such a doofus.

SAM. I have an idea...let's go to the dining room and see if we can find some sexy dames for you to practice on.

CLOVIS. Oh nooo...I'm not ready for that.

SAM. Well I think that sooner is better than later...most of them are hard of hearing anyway.

CLOVIS. OK Sam...whatever you say –

SAM. Now...write these down. *(Beat.)* Hey baby...ever done it in a Craftmatic adjustable bed?

CLOVIS. Oh...wow...I don't think I can say that one.

SAM. Yes you can...now write it down –

CLOVIS. OK Sam...you're the boss.

SAM. Now some of the others that have worked for me in the past –

(Their voices trail as they exit left. From Off stage we hear BEATRICE.)

BEATRICE. *(Offstage.)* OUCH...Watch where you're going... you stepped on my foot.

(EADDY, BEATRICE, IMOGENE and MAUDE enter right wearing an odd assortment of "protective gear" such as a bee-keepers hat with net, catcher's helmet, rubber dish gloves, football helmet, bicycle helmet etc. BEATRICE carries a fishing net on a pole. MAUDE carries a fly swatter. Her crown is on top of

her protective hat. **IMOGENE** *is wearing a portable oxygen tank and carries a baseball bat.* **EADDY** *wear binoculars around her neck and carries Little Peanut's cage. She also wears a fanny pack. She sits the cage down and peers through binoculars.)*

MAUDE. Do you see anything yet Eaddy?

IMOGENE, EADDY & BEATRICE. Shhhhhhhhh –

EADDY. You're gonna scare him off.

> (**IMOGENE** *sits on the bench and pulls out a flask from her bra and takes a drink.)*

IMOGENE. I can't believe I had to miss my hair appointment for this crap.

BEATRICE. Yeah...me too...but we can't expect Eaddy to go out into the wilderness alone and wrestle a wild animal to the ground.

MAUDE. Sounds like you on a hot Friday night Beatrice.

EADDY. Shut up and keep looking.

MAUDE. How did this happen? I just can't believe it.

EADDY. Oh please...you know exactly how this happened. The door to the cage and the window didn't just miraculously open on their own.

IMOGENE. What do you mean?

BEATRICE. It had to be that bitch Martha Parcell.

EADDY. She's always tries to do something to sabotage the other contestants. Remember when she tried to glue Tova Roberts to her chair with Super Glue?

MAUDE. Last year...she put itching powder in my panties. Remember?

EADDY. *(Scowl.)* Oh yes...that was just a true delight to see.

BEATRICE. *(Smirk.)* I think that this just might be the year that someone drops a house on 'ole Martha.

IMOGENE. Does anyone know what time Hazel will be back?

BEATRICE. *(Concern.)* Soon...too soon...

EADDY. Ladies...I think we need to pray.

BEATRICE. Not now Eaddy...I think we need –

EADDY. *(Stern.) Bow your head Jezebel*! Dear Lord... Please...help us as we search for Little Peanut...a precious and furry little orphan all alone in this cold and cruel world. I know I am undeserving Lord... particularly for the company I keep...with sinners, boozers...and sluts *(She gives "the side eye" to* **BEATRICE** *as her voice swells.)* But I know that in this, our most *desperate* hour of need –

> *(**MAUDE**, who has been peeking off into the distance sees something and stops* **EADDY***.)*

MAUDE. Look...look over there. Is that Little Peanut?

> *(**EADDY** looks through the binoculars.)*

EADDY. Yes...yes...OH THANK YOU LORD!

BEATRICE. Where?

EADDY. There...next to the hydrangea bush.

> *(**MAUDE** squints off into the distance.* **BEATRICE** *grabs the binoculars to look through them, choking* **EADDY** *in the process.* **EADDY** *pulls the binoculars away.)*

BEATRICE. Yeah...that's him alright.

IMOGENE. How do you know it's him?

EADDY. Well...for starters...it's the only squirrel wearing a little Christmas tutu.

IMOGENE. Yeah...that's definitely a good sign.

EADDY. Now we just need to get Little Peanut...back in this cage.

MAUDE. *(Excited.)* OOOOOOOOOOOOOOO...OK...what's the plan?

(Blank stares all around.)

EADDY. There is no plan. Do I *look* like I have a plan?

MAUDE. OK...listen...I say...Imogene and I sneak around behind him...and then get him to run this way. I'll be Thelma... Imogene you'll be Louise. Beatrice...you be ready with that net. Eaddy...open the cage...and be ready to *sling* him in there.

BEATRICE. No...that might scare him off. We're running out of time. I say...we just all rush him at once...and then Eaddy...you throw yourself on top of him.

IMOGENE. WHAT? We're not trying to kill him Beatrice.

EADDY. Enough! I've got this. He's tame y'all... I'll just casually walk over...and give him some of these pee-cans.

(EADDY unzips her fanny pack and pulls out a can of nuts. She shakes the can.)

Hey there Little Peanut...look what Auntie Eaddy has for you... I've got some super delicious pee-cans for you to nibble on...mmm mmm mmm –

IMOGENE. Oh...he sees us...I think he's coming over...be gentle...don't scare him –

(MAUDE suddenly points up, alarmed.)

MAUDE. *(Concern.)* Hey girls...what's that?

(EADDY squints up into the sky.)

EADDY. I don't know...what is that? Is it a kite?

BEATRICE. Who would be flying a kite at Magnolia Place?

IMOGENE. It looks awfully big...wait...it has wings...it looks like...like...a bird –

> (**EADDY** *hands* **BEATRICE** *the binoculars as the others continue to squint into the distance.*)

EADDY. A bird?

BEATRICE. Oh shit...OH SHIT!!! That's not a kite... THAT'S A HAWK!!!

MAUDE, IMOGENE & EADDY. A HAWK?

IMOGENE.	**BEATRICE.**
Oh no...is he –	Oh hell –

MAUDE. Run Little Peanut...RUN FOR YOUR LIFE!

> (*As the ladies stare in horror, the inevitable happens. They all gasp and scream bloody murder.* **MAUDE** *and* **BEATRICE** *duck for cover.* **IMOGENE** *swings her bat.* **EADDY** *grasps at air, as if she can save Little Peanut. Then, there is dead silence. As the ladies stand dumbstruck, a little Christmas tutu falls in front of them.* **BEATRICE** *picks it up and stares at it for a beat.*)

BEATRICE. Well. (*Beat.*) That's...unfortunate.

> (**MAUDE** *begins running in circles.*)

MAUDE. Help...help...help...someone...heeeellllpppp...call the police...call the National Guard...call –

> (**BEATRICE** *grabs* **MAUDE** *and slaps her... shaking her.*)

BEATRICE. SNAP OUT OF IT! Get yourself together.

EADDY. Hazel is going to kill me.

IMOGENE. No...*this* is gonna kill *her.*

MAUDE. What are we gonna do girls?

(There is a moment of silence.)

BEATRICE. I'll tell you what we're gonna do. Give me those binoculars.

> **(BEATRICE** *grabs the binoculars and begins scanning the courtyard.)*

MAUDE. *(Tearful.)* What are you looking for?

> **(BEATRICE** *spots her prey and points.)*

BEATRICE. THERE...*that's* what I'm looking for –

EADDY. *(Squinting.)* What...what is it?

IMOGENE. *(Realization.)* Oh no Beatrice...no –

EADDY. What? What is it?

IMOGENE. OH MY LORD...She's gonna try to catch another squirrel...a *wild* squirrel!

MAUDE. No...no she's not...*are you*?

BEATRICE. Duh...they all look alike. *(Beat.)* All we have to do is catch another squirrel...and put this little tutu on it. Hazel will never know the difference. *Look*...that one right there is perfect.

> *(They all peer into the distance...shaking their heads.)*

EADDY. Beatrice...I don't want to get into your personal business...but how exactly do you propose we catch a wild squirrel? Did you bring a dart gun?

BEATRICE. Well...I thought maybe we could go with Maude's...Thelma and Louise plan...and –

MAUDE. Oh...this is so exciting!

EADDY. This is never gonna work.

BEATRICE. It *has* to work...what other choice do we have? *(Beat.)* Give me those pee-cans...

IMOGENE. OK...I'm ready...let's do it –

>*(**IMOGENE** raises her bat. **BEATRICE** takes the pecans. She raises her fishing net high...and begins to shake the can.)*

BEATRICE. Eaddy...get ready with the cage.

>*(**EADDY** opens the cage and takes a baseball catchers stance.)*

OK girls...do your thing.

>*(**MAUDE** and **IMOGENE** begin to slowly step forward.)*

(Singsong.)

HERE LITTLE SQUIRREL SQUIRREL SQUIRREL...COME TO MAMA...I'VE GOT A DELICIOUS LITTLE SNACK FOR YOU –

>*(The others join in calling the squirrel.)*

>*(Blackout.)*

ACT II

Scene One

(Lights up on The Studio for "Senior Moments." There are two chairs. **EADDY** *attempts to fix the "Senior Moments" sign again using a piece of tape. It looks tacky but stays in place. Satisfied, she sits in the stage right chair and begins looking over her cue cards. Along with her normal pantsuit, she wears a fancy sequin and feathered hat, feather boa and large rhinestone earrings.)*

VOICE-OVER. OK Miss Clayton...let's do this please...settle please...we are LIVE ...in five, four, three, two, one... you're on –

(The peppy "Senior Moments" intro plays.)*

EADDY. Well hello Petula, Georgia...and welcome to Senior Moments...coming to you live from Magnolia Place Assisted Living. I'm your host...Eaddy May Clayton. Tonight is the Seventh Annual Miss Magnolia Senior Citizen Beauty Pageant...and I'm giving you all a sneak peek, behind the scenes look at all the glitz, glamour, and excitement. *(Beat.)* Lurleen Dupree was supposed

---

* A license to produce *The Miss Magnolia Senior Citizen Beauty Pageant* does not include a performance license for any third-party or copyrighted music. Licensees should create an original composition or use music in the public domain. For further information, please see the Music and Third-Party Materials Use Note on page iii.

to be with me today...but is once again *nowhere* to be found...so I –

(**LURLEEN** *rushes in and plops down in the other chair. She is oblivious to anything...and is rifling through her large and over filled tote.*)

LURLEEN. Sorry...sorry I'm late... I really didn't want to be here. *(Beat.)* When does this shindig start?

EADDY. *(Low.)* We're on *now* sweetie. *LIVE. (Then.)* And let's please welcome our special guest today...the always *fashionably* late...Lurleen Dupree.

(**LURLEEN** *glances up and waves into the camera, then returns to rifling through her purse.*)

LURLEEN. Oh...okay...whatever...hey y'all –

(**EADDY** *shakes her head and sighs.*)

EADDY. So...Lurleen, tell us a little about how you put together this glamourous pageant.

(**LURLEEN** *is not paying attention. Her purse rifling becomes more frantic.*)

Lurleen dear...I don't want to get into your personal business...but what are you looking for?

(**LURLEEN** *suddenly pulls out a pill bottle and raises it victoriously into the air.*)

LURLEEN. OH, THANK GOD!! I found them!

EADDY. Found what?

LURLEEN. My Valium.

EADDY. *(Grimace.)* Ah yes...another exclusive, behind the scenes look at the secret world of pageantry. *(Then defeated.)* Valium.

(**LURLEEN** *is desperately trying to get the pill bottle open, clawing, chewing and banging the bottle. She finally gets it open and pops a pill into her mouth.*)

LURLEEN. Dang it...I broke the cap...here...hold this.

EADDY. Well...I...was hoping you might tell the viewers –

(**LURLEEN** *thrusts the bottle and broken cap into* **EADDY'S** *hands and pulls out a beverage cup from her tote. She takes a huge gulp to wash down the pill. Her cell phone rings, and she answers.*)

LURLEEN. Hello, Lurleen speaking –

EADDY. Lurleen sugar...we are on the air!

LURLEEN. WHAT???? Nooo...I need that for tomorrow night!

EADDY. Lurleen please –

LURLEEN. *(Oblivious.)* I cannot believe that I have let myself get dragged into throwing this damn pageant again...every year I say it's the last one...but *nooo*... here I am *AGAIN* trying to wrangle together something decent for these crabby old broads...and then next weekend I've got to deal with all those snotty little pre-teen bimbos...it's no wonder I'm poppin' Valium left and right –

(**EADDY** *rises and steps toward the "camera" and leans in as* **LURLEEN** *turns away and quietly ad-lib gripes into her phone.*)

EADDY. *(Strained.)* Well...why don't we take a little break now...and hear from our newest show sponsor...The Happy Hooker...for all your bait and tackle needs. *(Beat.)* Go to commercial! *(Beat.)* Are we off the air?

VOICE-OVER. Yes

EADDY. Thank you Lord! Hey...can somebody throw on the episode where Vera takes off her top...that's always a favorite...I'm out of here.

>(**LURLEEN** *continues to ad-lib argue as* **EADDY** *exits.*)

>(*Blackout.*)

Scene Two

(Lights up in the Day Room. **CLOVIS** *is wearing a funky outfit with a bright patterned shirt which is unbuttoned low, a gold chain and tight pants. He still wears his nerdy glasses.* **SAM** *is checking out his handywork and holding a flashy biker jacket for* **CLOVIS**.*)*

SAM. OK...try this jacket.

*(**SAM** helps **CLOVIS** into a cool biker jacket.)*

CLOVIS. I don't know about this Sam. Are you sure this look is me?

SAM. Oh yeah...we just need to get rid of those glasses... and put these on and you'll be all set.

CLOVIS. I can't see without my glasses.

SAM. Eh...who cares...that will just make the ladies even better looking. Try these.

*(**SAM** gives **CLOVIS** a cool pair of sunglasses. **CLOVIS** takes off his glasses and puts on the sunglasses.)*

CLOVIS. Whatever you say Sam...you're the boss.

SAM. Now show me that walk.

*(**CLOVIS** demonstrates a much-improved walk.)*

CLOVIS. How's that?

SAM. Great! *Really* good. I'm a miracle worker! Now hit me with one of those pickup lines.

*(**CLOVIS** takes a confident stance.)*

CLOVIS.   Hey baby...wanna see the size of my...social security check? *(He does the finger gun point and chick chick sound.)*

SAM. Oh yeah...you're ready. My work here is done.

> *(CLOVIS takes off the sunglasses and puts his eyeglasses back on.)*

CLOVIS. Well...maybe not...I –

> *(Enter HAZEL carrying Little Peanut's cage. She is passing through.)*

HAZEL. Bad boy, Little Peanut!!! Why did you bite me... that hurt...what is wrong with you?

> *(The cage jerks from side to side as she begins to sing.)*

SILENT NIGHT...HOLY NIGHT...ALL IS CALM...ALL IS... OUCH!!!!!

> *(HAZEL exits.)*

SAM. What do you mean Clovis? You've got the look...the walk...the best pick-up lines...what else do you need?

CLOVIS.   Well...this is awkward...but...uh...if all this works...what do I do next? I mean...after what happened yesterday in the dining room...I –

SAM. *(Reassuring.)* Don't worry...Doctor Head said that Lucille will regain the sight in her eye...in a week or so.

CLOVIS. Oh good...that's a relief.

SAM. Yeah...so...I thought this question might come up. Have a seat.

> *(CLOVIS sits on the sofa as SAM pulls a life-sized inflatable woman doll from behind the sofa. The doll wears a negligee and fishnets.)*

SAM. OK...I got this for you to practice with. It's called Inflate-A-Date.

CLOVIS. Um...I'm desperate Sam...but I'm not *that* desperate.

SAM. No no...this is just to practice the moves.

CLOVIS. The moves?

SAM. Yeah...just pretend this is your date. Now...it's the end of the night...and you're parked outside...or maybe...if you're lucky...she's invited you back to her room. What do you do?

> *(Beat.)*

CLOVIS. *(Scowling.)* I don't think I would date anyone that looks like this...she looks a little trashy.

> (SAM *"sits" the doll by* CLOVIS *on the sofa.* CLOVIS *stares at it.)*

SAM. We're just pretending.

CLOVIS. Does she have a name?

SAM. Uh...yeah...her name is Lou Lou...now put your arm around her.

> (CLOVIS *adjusts his glasses and then scoots over by the doll.)*

CLOVIS. I'm nervous.

SAM. Try to do the yawn and stretch move...and then put your arm around her...you know...like this.

> (SAM *mimes the yawn and stretch...raising his arm and showing how to put it around his date.)*

CLOVIS. OK...yeah...I've seen that in the movies. Like this?

(**CLOVIS** *does a perfect yawn and stretch. His hand resting on Lou Lou's bosom. He nonchalantly begins to caress the bosom.*)

SAM.   Yes Clovis...perfect...now you're in the perfect position to ease in for a little midnight smooch.

(**CLOVIS** *suddenly gasps and pulls his arm away...jumping up.*)

CLOVIS.   Oh no...I'm sorry...I'm sorry.

SAM.   *(Alarmed.)* WHAT??

CLOVIS.   *(Distressed.)* I TOUCHED LOU LOU'S BOSOM!

SAM.   Calm down Clovis. It's just a bag full of air.

CLOVIS.   Oh yeah right...right...sorry.

SAM.   Now try again...and this time...lean in for a little romantic kiss.

(**SAM** *holds the doll in place as* **CLOVIS** *does the yawn and stretch move...then closes his eyes, puckers up and leans in for a kiss. At that very moment,* **BEATRICE** *enters wearing her very distinctive feather trimmed robe. She carries a piece of sequin costume for the pageant.*)

Yeah...that's real good CLOVIS...you got the moves man...go for it...yeah...GO FOR IT!

(**BEATRICE** *is intrigued and slowly crosses to the sofa...as* **CLOVIS** *pulls in the doll and kisses it passionately, grabbing its rear end.*)

BEATRICE.   *What in the hell* are y'all doing in here?

(**CLOVIS** *screams and falls back onto the sofa.* **SAM** *yells and launches the doll across the room.*)

SAM. Hey Beatrice...we were just...uh...practicing our... uh...CPR training.

CLOVIS. Uh...yeah...right...CPR.

BEATRICE. I don't think CPR involves tongue.

(**BEATRICE** *laughs and crosses to exit.*)

The girls are never gonna believe this.

(**SAM** *crosses to* **BEATRICE.**)

SAM. Wait Beatrice...do you think you could keep this... just between us? You know...*friend to friend*?

BEATRICE. Oh *no way*...this is *top shelf* gossip.

(**CLOVIS** *rises and sheepishly crosses to* **BEATRICE.**)

CLOVIS. Excuse me...Miss Beatrice...please don't tell anyone about this. I mean...I don't think I would live this down... I would just be too humiliated... I might have to move out of here...or even move out of state.

BEATRICE. *(Flirty.)* OK sugar pot...I'm feelin' generous today...so mums the word.

(**BEATRICE** *pinches* **CLOVIS**'s *bottom.* **CLOVIS** *gasps.*)

Oh Sam...are you performing your Elvis act tonight at the pageant?

SAM. Yeah...sure am.

(**BEATRICE** *crosses to exit and then turns back seductively.*)

BEATRICE. Great...can't wait...and by the way...good work with your little protégé there...he's almost on *my* radar.

(**BEATRICE** *winks and blows a kiss at* **CLOVIS** *and exits.* **SAM** *gives* **CLOVIS** *a high five.*)

CLOVIS. Wow...she pinched my bottom.

SAM. Clovis...man...you just got the Beatrice Shelton Seal of Approval. *(Beat.)* I mean...don't get too excited... she has *really* low standards. Her only requirements for a date are two legs and a zipper *(Beat.)* the legs are optional.

CLOVIS. So, what is this about your *Elvis act*?

SAM. I'm doing my old Vegas routine tonight, to entertain the audience in between the evening gown part and the talent part. I do it every year. The ladies go crazy!

CLOVIS. Oh man...I can't wait to see that.

SAM. *(Lightbulb.)* Hey...I have a great idea.

(**SAM** *crosses to* **CLOVIS** *and gives him the once over.*)

I know how we can reveal the new you. Can you dance?

CLOVIS. Uh...I don't know...I've never tried...*why*?

SAM. I AM BRILLIANT *(Then.)* Clovis my man...how's your pelvic thrust?

CLOVIS. My *what*?

(Blackout.)

Scene Three

(An hour later in the day room...which is being used as a dressing room. It's hectic. MARTHA, BEATRICE, EADDY, HAZEL and IMOGENE prepare for the pageant. Everyone is wearing robes, hairnets etc. BEATRICE is wearing her very distinctive feather trimmed robe. The rolling rack of glitz is upstage. There are a couple of TV trays with makeup, mirrors, hairspray etc. HAZEL has large white blood stained bandages on several fingers. She peeks into Little Peanut's cage, which has a cover on it. MARTHA has a hand mirror and is attempting to look at herself from every angle as she paces.)

HAZEL. It's OK Little Peanut...just calm down darlin'... I know you're nervous.

MARTHA. That rodent is smelling up the dressing room.

HAZEL. He is not!

BEATRICE. Martha you are such a bitch –

MARTHA. Cursing like a sailor is not very lady like.

BEATRICE. Neither is your mustache.

> *(MARTHA looks in the mirror panicked, then scowls.)*

MARTHA. Sounds like someone is feeling the pressure.

BEATRICE. I'll show you pressure...with my hands around your neck.

> *(BEATRICE attempts to cross to MARTHA. IMOGENE stops her.)*

IMOGENE. Stop it you two... I mean it...my nerves are shot.

EADDY. I can't believe I am doing this.

HAZEL. I love doing things like this...it makes me feel... young and *vital*.

EADDY. Vital? Yeah right! I see all these *"vital"* seniors out there going hiking and taking dance lessons...and I'm just happy if I can get both feet into my panties without losing my balance and falling over.

> (**HAZEL** *picks up the cage and it begins to jerk and shake.*)

HAZEL. OOOOO...it's okay Little Peanut...he's so nervous –

> (**HAZEL** *begins to sing "Away in a Manger."* **IMOGENE, EADDY** *and* **BEATRICE** *all react nervously.*)

BEATRICE. Maybe you ought to let him sit this one out...he seems...uh...a little...*agitated*.

EADDY.	**IMOGENE.**
Oh yes –	I agree...agitated –

HAZEL. Oh nooo...we have practiced and practiced. He'll be fine...he just has the jitters.

MARTHA. *(Not thinking.)* I still can't believe you *actually* found him –

> (**IMOGENE, EADDY** *and* **BEATRICE** *freeze and turn to* **HAZEL**.)

HAZEL. *(Confused.)* Found him? What are you talking about?

MARTHA. *(Caught.)* I mean...you know...found him...uh... that you *found* a squirrel for a pet.

HAZEL. Yes...he is my precious baby.

> (*The cage jerks violently in her hands.*)

I think he just needs a little nap before the pageant starts. I'll see you girls in a bit. I'm gonna let him rest quietly in my room.

> (EADDY, IMOGENE *and* BEATRICE *ad-lib mumble.* HAZEL *exits singing "Away in a Manger" as the cage jerks violently.*)

EADDY.	IMOGENE.	BEATRICE.
OK.	See ya soon.	Good luck fruit loop.

> (BEATRICE, EADDY *and* IMOGENE *all turn and give* MARTHA *a death stare.*)

MARTHA. Well...then...uh... I'm going to go put on my costume and practice one more time...not that I need it...this *will* be my year.

> (MARTHA *looks at herself in the hand mirror and fishes for a compliment.*)

Ugh...when did I get so old and fat?

> (MARTHA *exits.*)

BEATRICE. *(Calling out.)* At least your still have your eyesight!

IMOGENE. Can you believe the gall of that woman?

EADDY. Oh...she knows that we know she let Little Peanut out.

BEATRICE. And she knows...that we know that she knows. We can't let her get away with this.

IMOGENE. But what can we do? We don't have any real proof.

EADDY. Ooooo...the thought of that woman winning this pageant...just makes want to commit a sin...and I'm talking one of the top ten –

IMOGENE. That *cannot* happen.

EADDY. What are we gonna do...lock her in a closet?

IMOGENE. She would just claw her way out...she's *nothing* if not determined.

> (**BEATRICE** *crosses down...she has a devious idea.*)

BEATRICE. Well...what if she became...*incapacitated*...and couldn't be in the pageant?

EADDY. Incapacitated?

BEATRICE. You know...like...if something unexpected happened...and she had to sit this one out.

EADDY. There's not a chance of that happening...she is obsessed with winning.

BEATRICE. Hey Eaddy...didn't you have a bottle of Lurleen's Valium earlier?

EADDY. *(No clue.)* Oh yes...thanks for reminding me...the cap broke...so I poured it in an aspirin bottle. I'm going to give them back to her when I –

IMOGENE. Oh no –

BEATRICE. Where is it?

IMOGENE. Oh no –

EADDY. I have them right here in my makeup case, so I won't forget to – *(Beat.)* Wait...why?

BEATRICE. Give them to me.

> (**EADDY** *pulls out an aspirin bottle and* **BEATRICE** *takes it.*)

BEATRICE. I know exactly what we can do with these.

IMOGENE. Oooooo noooooo...we're all going to jail –

EADDY. Wait...are you talking about drugging Martha?

BEATRICE. Oh no...no...not *drugging her*...just...you know...*relaxing* her...*(Dry.) a lot.*

(**EADDY** *begins to pray in a panic.*)

EADDY. Dear Lord...please do not strike me with lightning. I promise that I will not be a part of this wicked and devious plot. I am just an innocent bystander Lord... and would never –

IMOGENE & BEATRICE. EADDY!

(**LURLEEN** *enters. She is a nervous wreck. She wears a robe and house shoes and has put her hair up, using a fancy clip in hairpiece. She is muttering to herself as she enters. She crosses to the costume rack and begins pawing angrily at the dresses.*)

LURLEEN. Every year...*EVERY* year...I say...this is the last one...this is the last time...but noooooo...here I am... *AGAIN*! Why do I do this to myself?

EADDY. Lurleen honey...are you okay?

IMOGENE. You look a little...frazzled.

LURLEEN. Frazzled? *FRAZZLED*? Yes I'm *frazzled*... I got a run in my best control top pantyhose... I'm getting a migraine...and *(Tearful.)* I can't find my Valium.

EADDY. Oh honey, calm down...I've got –

(**BEATRICE** *grabs* **EADDY**'s *arm and scowls at her.*)

LURLEEN. You've got what?

BEATRICE. Aspirin...she's got aspirin –

EADDY. Yes...I've got...an aspirin if you need it.

LURLEEN. *(Incredulous.)* Aspirin? Really? Do you have a bottle of Jack Daniels to wash it down with? This

pageant is gonna be the death of me. Every year...
EVERY year...I say...this is the last one...this is the last
time –

> (**LURLEEN** *grabs her evening gown off the rack
> and exits upstage center as* **MAUDE** *enters
> wearing a bathrobe, shower cap, crown, and
> flip flops. She has a little pair of spray tan
> protection eye goggles on, pushed up on her
> forehead.*)

MAUDE. Hey girls...is anyone else getting a spray tan? All
the beauty queens do it ya know.

BEATRICE. Sorry...but we're plotting...er uh...planning
something special for tonight.

MAUDE. What is it? OOOO is it for me?

IMOGENE. Uh...yes...of course –

EADDY. Now you don't want to ruin the surprise do you?
Now shoo...

MAUDE. OH...you girls are too sweet...well...if you want to
get a spray tan...Nelda from Malibu Glow On The Go
Tan, is set up out in the parking lot...she's one of the
sponsors...and it's free.

BEATRICE. *(Abrupt.)* Great...thanks for letting us know...
well...bye.

> (**MAUDE** *gives them a happy look and shakes
> her head.*)

MAUDE. You girls...you are just too too sweet to me.

> (**MAUDE** *exits.* **EADDY** *turns to* **BEATRICE** *and
> grabs the pill bottle.*)

EADDY. Give me those...have you just completely lost your
mind? Now you can just forget it...we are not drugging
Martha...and that's final!

(**EADDY** *puts the bottle of Valium back into her makeup case.*)

BEATRICE. PARTY POOPER!

IMOGENE. OK...well...I'm gonna go find Sam. I haven't seen him all day...and I need to make sure the geriatric floozies around here are keeping their hands off!

(**IMOGENE** *crosses to the upstage center arch then turns back.*)

When he gets in that Elvis costume...they just get to pantin' after him like dogs in heat.

(**IMOGENE** *exits upstage center.*)

BEATRICE. OK...well...uh...I'm just gonna run back to my room. I forgot my...uh...false eyelashes. You need anything?

EADDY. No...thank you.

(**BEATRICE** *crosses left, eyeing* **EADDY** *suspiciously and then exits stage left. When* **EADDY** *is alone, she takes the Valium from her makeup case and pours a pill into her hand and puts the bottle back. She looks up.*)

I know...I know...don't look at me like that. I'll ask forgiveness later.

(**EADDY** *quickly exits stage right. Seconds later,* **IMOGENE** *peeks in from upstage center and crosses to* **EADDY**'s *makeup case, takes out the bottle and pockets two pills.*)

IMOGENE. Two should be enough.

(**IMOGENE** *puts the bottle back and scurries out upstage center. A few seconds later,* **BEATRICE** *peeks in from stage left and then crosses to* **EADDY**'s *makeup case, takes out the* *bottle and dumps the remaining pills into her hand.)*

BEATRICE. Two, four, six...hmmmm...four should be enough.

*(**BEATRICE** drops two pills back into the bottle, closes it and drops it back into the makeup case.)*

And two for Lurleen.

(Blackout.)

Scene Four

(Peppy pageant style music plays*. At half lights, the crew is quickly setting up for the pageant. In the dim light we hear a very frazzled **LURLEEN**.)

LURLEEN. If we could just get this done sometime today! *(Mutter.)* Every year...every year I say I'm not doing this crap again...but noooooo here I am...once again... slinging together a pageant for a bunch of old –

(A spotlight begins to sweep wildly across the stage and then settles on **LURLEEN**. *Lights up.* **LURLEEN** *is stage right standing at a podium. She immediately goes from a frown to a big smile. Beside her is a small table with a boom box, a MISS MAGNOLIA sash, three small trophies, three envelopes and a bundle of flowers. stage left is an easel with the poster advertising The Belle of the Ball Evening Wear Emporium. A cheap gold shiny mylar curtain backdrop that serves as the "stage" for the pageant stands center. A sign that reads GOLDEN OLDIES is mounted at the top of the mylar curtain.* **LURLEEN** *presses a button on the boom box, stopping the music abruptly.)*

Good evening ladies and gentlemen and welcome to the Seventh Annual *(Then aside.)* Oh God...has it been *seven* years? *(Then.)* Seventh Annual Miss Magnolia Senior Citizen Beauty Pageant. This year's theme is GOLDEN OLDIES. I am sorry to announce that one

---

* A licence to produce *The Miss Magnolia Senior Citizen Beauty Pageant* does not include a performance licence for any third-party or copyrighted music. Licensees should create an original composition or use music in the public domain. For further information, please see the Music and Third-Party Materials Use Note on page iii.

of our sponsors, Malibu Glow on the Go Spray Tanning has been removed from sponsoring the pageant due to an unfortunate...um...incident...out in parking lot earlier this afternoon.

LURLEEN. *Now...*tonight, our five golden oldies will be competing in evening gown and talent categories. We also have some special entertainment lined up. *(Beat.)* Unfortunately, we couldn't put together the opening number we had planned. However, our reigning Miss Magnolia, Maude Jenkins has graciously agreed to reprise her award-winning talent from last year's pageant...despite an...uh...unfortunate *incident* earlier this afternoon. *(Beat.)* What a trooper. So please...put your hands together and welcome our current reigning Miss Magnolia Senior Citizen... Ms. Maude Jenkins!!

> *(**LURLEEN** holds up an "Applause" sign and starts the music on the boom box. **MAUDE** enters. She is dressed from head to toe as Shirley Temple in a sailor dress, sailor hat, ringlet curls wig, knee socks and tap shoes. Her face, arms and legs are smeared and streaked with orange. She carries a large, swirled lollypop. She launches into a costume appropriate tap dance routine. She clomps and stomps around the stage joyfully... attempting several steps and moves. She is dreadful. A wide-eyed **LURLEEN** stops the music early and encourages the audience to applaud. **MAUDE** frowns but takes a bow.)*

MAUDE. Thank you...thank you to all the little people. It's good to be queen!

> *(**MAUDE** exits.)*

LURLEEN. Weellll now...wasn't that just...*somethin'* *(Beat.)* So...let's go ahead and get this show on the road. Shall we? Each of our contestants is modeling a gorgeous evening gown from the *gently used* Nifty and Thrifty section in *my* boutique...Belle of the Ball Evening Wear Emporium...where we have elegance and glamour for every budget...even the cheap people. So...let's give them all a round of applause...OK?

> (**LURLEEN** *pops in another tape and a light instrumental pageant walk plays. She holds up an "Applause" sign.*)

LURLEEN.   Contestant number one is Ms. Eaddy Mae Clayton.

> (**EADDY** *enters. She is nervous and awkward. She mumbles "Elbow, Elbow, Wrist, Wrist" as she models.*)

Eaddy is a six-year resident of Magnolia Place...a member of the Petula First Baptist Church and Vice President of The Senior Gals on The Go and the host of the Senior Moments talk show on Cable Access 14. She enjoys macramé, quilting, praying, and reading her Bible. Let's have a round of applause for contestant number one...Eaddy Mae Clayton...thank you Eaddy... lovely...just lovely.

> (**EADDY** *exits.*)

Now let's welcome Contestant Number Two... Ms. Beatrice Shelton.

> (**BEATRICE** *enters. She is bold. She flirts and shimmies. She fans herself with a feather fan.*)

Beatrice is a seven-year resident of Magnolia Place and is the activities director for The Senior Gals on the Go. She enjoys meeting new men and...*(Beat.)* wait...*I'm not* reading this –

BEATRICE.   *(Still modeling.)* Just read it!

LURLEEN. No –

BEATRICE. *(Sharp.)* READ IT!

LURLEEN. Fine...*(Blurt.)*...meeting new men...and is available day or night for hot and sexy fun. Stop by apartment 3B...no invitation necessary. *(Beat.)* Lord have mercy...we are all going to hell. *(Compose.)* Thank you contestant number two... Slutty Shelton...I mean... Beatrice...Ms. Beatrice Shelton.

> **(BEATRICE** *turns and looks over her shoulder, wiggling her bottom.)*

BEATRICE. Come and get me boys!!

> **(BEATRICE** *exits as several men whistle and cat call.)*

LURLEEN. Now...let's welcome contestant number three... Ms. Martha Parcell.

> **(MARTHA** *enters. She seems slightly out of it... but manages to get through.)*

Martha is an eight-year resident of Magnolia Place and leader of the canasta club. Her hobbies include knitting, baking, and following local crime on her old police scanner...oooo fun.

> **(MARTHA** *smiles and waves in a daze, then attempts to exit in the wrong direction.)*

You're going the wrong way darlin'.

> **(MARTHA** *stops and looks around bewildered.)*

MARTHA. I knew that.

LURLEEN. Well...let's have a nice round of applause for contestant number three...Martha Parcell.

MARTHA. IT'S *MY* YEAR!!

(**MARTHA** *exits.*)

LURLEEN. *(Fake smile.)* Precious. *(Beat.)* OK then...let's welcome to the stage our next contestant...contestant number four...Ms. Hazel Dillard.

> (**HAZEL** *enters. She now has a large Band-Aid on her forehead. Her walker is decorated for Christmas.*)

Hazel is a two-year resident of Magnolia Place. She is the president and only member of the Petula Squirrel Lovers Association. Her hobbies include wrapping Christmas gifts and Christmas caroling year-round. Thank you, contestant number four...Hazel Dillard.

> (**HAZEL** *exits.*)

And now let's welcome our fifth and final contestant... Ms. Imogene Smith.

> (**IMOGENE** *enters pulling her oxygen tank. The tank is decorated to match her gown.*)

Imogene is a one-year resident of Magnolia Place. She is the secretary of The Senior Gals on the Go...and –

> (**IMOGENE** *is tangled in her oxygen hose.*)

Um...do you need some help honey?

IMOGENE. No...I've got this –

> (**LURLEEN** *steps forward to help* **IMOGENE**.)

LURLEEN. Here let me –

IMOGENE. I'VE GOT IT!!!

> (**LURLEEN** *backs away as* **IMOGENE** *composes herself.*)

LURLEEN. Okay then...sorry...Imogene enjoys gardening and long walks in the park with her husband Sam Smith...and she wants all the ladies in the audience to know that they need to keep their hands off her husband...or she will break your fingers.

IMOGENE. *(Smiling.)* With a hammer –

> *(Uneasy beat.)*

LURLEEN. Well...how about that? Thank you...contestant number five...Imogene Smith.

> **(IMOGENE** *exits.* **LURLEEN** *stops the music.)*

Let's have another big round of applause for all our... GOLDEN OLDIES!

> **(LURLEEN** *holds up the "Applause" sign.)*

Well...it looks like it's gonna be a stiff competition this year. *(Beat.)* Now...while the ladies are changing into their talent costumes...let's welcome to the stage... OH and ladies...remember...hands off unless you want broken fingers...let's welcome Magnolia Place resident and former Las Vegas stud muffin...Sam Smith...as ELVIS PRESLEY!!

SAM. *(Offstage.)* WAIT...wait –

> **(SAM***'s arm pokes through the mylar curtain holding an index card.)*

LURLEEN. What? Okaaayyy.

> **(LURLEEN** *crosses and takes the card and looks it over quickly.)*

Well...okay then...how about that...just a slight change in plans...let's welcome to the stage...Sam Smith *and* Clovis Crown...as THE DUELING ELVISES

(LURLEEN starts the music.* SAM enters through the curtain dressed as Elvis...in a jumpsuit, cape, Elvis wig, and sunglasses. He begins lip-syncing to a peppy tune. After the first verse, he steps to the side and gestures to the curtain. CLOVIS enters in full Elvis regalia. At first...he is a little awkward and his lip-sync is off...but then he really let's loose and dances. SAM joins in and there is a bit of synchronized dancing, karate chops and kicks, ending in a hysterical pose. BEATRICE runs on wearing the very distinctive feather trimmed robe over her costume and throws a pair of bright red panties, then exits. CLOVIS picks them up. He looks at SAM.)

CLOVIS. This is so unsanitary.

(CLOVIS throws down the panties.)

SAM. Just bow doofus...BOW.

(SAM and CLOVIS bow together. LURLEEN holds up the "Applause" sign.)

LURLEEN. Wasn't that...just...precious. Come on...let's give it up one more time for our dueling Elvises! WOOO! Thanks guys.

(SAM exits...but CLOVIS continues to bow until SAM returns to drag him off. CLOVIS runs back out and grabs the panties and exits.)

Alright everyone...sorry about that...let's settle down. It's time for these beautiful contestants to show you

---

*A license to produce *The Miss Magnolia Senior Citizen Beauty Pageant* does not include a performance license for any third-party or copyrighted music. Licensees should create an original composition or use music in the public domain. For further information, please see the Music and Third-Party Materials Use Note on page iii.

their talent...if they have any. OK...so let's welcome our first contestant, Ms. Eaddy Mae Clayton...who will dazzle us with her amazing ventriloquist skills...oooo fun.

> (**EADDY** *enters. She is wearing a church choir robe. Her arm is behind her back. She blows into a pitch pipe and sings a note or two trying to get on pitch. She fails.*)

EADDY. *(Multiple notes.)* Thiiis...thiiiiisss little...thiiiiis –

> (**EADDY** *settles on a note and sings the first line and then out pops her puppet. The puppet is also wearing a choir robe.* **EADDY** *attempts to change her voice and sings out of the side of her mouth. She is a terrible ventriloquist.*)

THIS LITTLE LIGHT OF MINE... I'M GONNA LET IT SHINE.

PUPPET.
THIS LITTLE LIGHT OF MINE... I'M GONNA LET IT SHINE.

EADDY.
THIS LITTLE LIGHT OF MINE... I'M GONNA LET IT SHINE.

PUPPET.
LET IT SHINE, ALL THE TIME, LET IT SHIIIIIIIIIINE!

EADDY.
HIDE IT UNDER A BUSHEL --

PUPPET.
NO! I'M GONNA LET IT SHINE.

EADDY.
HIDE IT UNDER A BUSHEL --

PUPPET.
NO! I'M GONNA LET IT SHINE.

EADDY.
HIDE IT UNDER A BUSHEL --

PUPPET.

NO! I'M GONNA LET IT SHINE.

EADDY.

LET IT SHINE...LET IT SHINE

PUPPET.

LET IT SHINE!

> (**EADDY** *really gets into the last verse...*
> *encouraging people to clap and sing along.*)

EADDY. All right everybody...let's get those hands together.
Sing along with me...OK?

ALL AROUND MAGNOLIA PLACE... I'M GONNA LET IT
SHINE.

PUPPET.

ALL AROUND MAGNOLIA PLACE... I'M GONNA LET IT
SHINE.

EADDY.

ALL AROUND MAGNOLIA PLACE... I'M GONNA LET IT
SHINE.

PUPPET.

LET IT SHINE... LET IS SHINE... OH YEAH BABY... I'M
GONNA LET IT SHIIIIIIIINNNNNEEEEEEE!

> (**LURLEEN** *turns off the music and then holds*
> *up the "Applause" sign.* **EADDY** *bows and*
> *smiles.*)

LURLEEN. Weeellll...praise the Lord and pass the peas.
Thank you contestant number one...Eaddy Mae
Clayton. Wasn't she just awesome? You could hardly
see her mouth moving...if you didn't look directly at it.
Just precious.

> (**EADDY** *exits through the curtain.* **LURLEEN**
> *picks up the next cue card.*)

LURLEEN. Well...alright then...our next contestant... number two is...Ms. Beatrice Shelton...who will be performing...uh...

> (**LURLEEN** *flips the cue card over.*)

Hmmm...it doesn't say on here what she's doing. *(Loud.)* MS. SHELTON...YOU NEVER TOLD ME WHAT YOU'RE DOING FOR YOUR TALENT HON –

BEATRICE. *(Offstage.)* IT'S A SURPRISE!

LURLEEN. Oh...okay...a surprise...well...let's hope for the best then...and welcome to the stage...Ms. Beatrice Shelton doing a *surprise* talent.

> (**LURLEEN** *starts the music and a bawdy bump and grind burlesque tune plays.*[*] **BEATRICE** *enters wearing a sexy gown, long gloves, boa, and feathered headpiece. She begins to shimmy and shoulder roll. She drops and drags her boa, doing a sexy turn and hip swivel.*)

Oh goodness...Ms. Shelton...I'm not sure this is –

> (**BEATRICE** *peels off a glove and twirls it over her head, throwing it at* **LURLEEN**. *We hear a few cat calls and whistles from the back of the room.*)

Um...Ms. Shelton...this is not appropriate.

> (**BEATRICE** *peels off the other glove and twirls it over her head, throwing it at* **LURLEEN**. *We hear a cat call.*)

---

[*] A license to produce *The Miss Magnolia Senior Citizen Beauty Pageant* does not include a performance license for any third-party or copyrighted music. Licensees should create an original composition or use music in the public domain. For further information, please see the Music and Third-Party Materials Use Note on page iii. .

Ms. Shelton...I'm gonna have to ask you to not take anything else off dear. Please don't –

> (**BEATRICE** *turns her back and unzips her dress. She drops the dress to reveal a black slip. She quickly turns to reveal tassel pasties on the breasts.* **LURLEEN** *stops the music and rushes over and drags* **BEATRICE** *through the curtain.*)

Whew...that was close. *(Then.)* I'm so sorry y'all...some things can never be unseen.

BEATRICE. *(Offstage.)* I was just getting to the good part!

> *(Cat calls and whistles.)*

OK...calm down...now...let's see who we have next. *(Beat.)* Ah...next we have contestant number three... Ms. Martha Parcell and her Flameless Fire Batons. Let's have a nice round of applause for Ms. Martha Parcell.

> (**LURLEEN** *holds up the applause sign and then starts a disco song.* No one comes out. She turns down the volume and speaks louder.*)

SO...LET'S WELCOME...MARTHA PARCELL AND HER FLAMELESS FIRE BATONS.

> *(There is another beat...and then* **LURLEEN** *stops the music.)*

OK then...something must be happening backstage... so we'll just move on to our next contestant.

---

* A license to produce *The Miss Magnolia Senior Citizen Beauty Pageant* does not include a performance license for any third-party or copyrighted music. Licensees should create an original composition or use music in the public domain. For further information, please see the Music and Third-Party Materials Use Note on page iii. .

(*A* **STAGEHAND** *yells from off stage.*)

STAGEHAND. She's coming...start the music.

LURLEEN. *(Flustered.)* Oh...okay...great...so much for getting home early –

> (**LURLEEN** *restarts the music.* **MARTHA** *enters. Her costume is on backwards and her number is on her back. She is a wide-eyed train wreck. Her lipstick is smeared across her face. She holds a baton with construction paper flames glued to the ends. She slurs as she talks to the audience.*)

MARTHA. This is my year. *(Beat.)* That woman wouldn't let me have real fire batons. *(Beat.)* Is it hot in here? I feel hot. Are you hot? *(She reaches out bewildered.)* Is this real life? *(Beat.)* Where am I?

LURLEEN. Honey...I think you may need to –

> (**MARTHA**'s *twirling is basically waving the baton back and forth and swirling her wrists. She attempts to toss the baton into the air and catch it. It falls to the ground. She tries to balance it on her head, and it falls. She bends over to get the baton. She stands back up disoriented with her back to the audience.*)

MARTHA. *(Loud.)* Where did everybody go?

> (**LURLEEN** *steps out and turns her around.*)

LURLEEN. Sweetie...do I need to get a nurse? Are you having an episode?

MARTHA. *(Laughing maniacally.)* Oh...there you are.

> (**MARTHA** *grabs a second baton from the floor and begins to jump around, kick and and then finishes her routine with a booty shake and a pitiful attempt at a split. With the*

music still playing, she bows and then starts to lay on the floor.)

I need a nap.

(LURLEEN stops the music.)

LURLEEN. Oh...okay...you're finished...NO Miss Parcell... get up...wait...you can't nap right now darlin'.

(MARTHA squints and staggers forward.)

MARTHA. IT'S MY YEAR!

(MARTHA wanders off stage.)

LURLEEN. *(Sarcastic.)* Yes...I believe you've mentioned that...and wasn't that just...uh...*original? (Beat.)* Now... let's see...that brings us to our next contestant...Miss Hazel Dillard and Little Peanut...performing a duet of "Jingle Bells."

(LURLEEN starts the karaoke music for "Jingle Bells." Then...there is a loud, terrified scream and a crash off stage. A crazed HAZEL rushes in. She is screaming and flailing her arms. She has a squirrel wearing a Santa suit and holding a tiny tambourine mounted on her face.)

HAZEL. Somebody heeeelp...help me...Little Peanut... BAD BOY...you're hurting mommy!

LURLEEN. WHAT IN BEAUTY QUEEN HELL?

HAZEL. Help me!!! Somebody HELP ME!!!!

(HAZEL runs toward LURLEEN.)

---

*A license to produce *The Miss Magnolia Senior Citizen Beauty Pageant* does not include a performance license for any third-party or copyrighted recordings. Licensees should create their own.

LURLEEN. Armageddon...ARMAGEDDON! Ahhhhhhhhh!!!

(The music continues to play as **LURLEEN** *runs across the stage and then off through the curtain screaming...followed closely by* **HAZEL.** *There is another crash and then* **LURLEEN** *reappears with Little Peanut now attached to her face followed closely by* **HAZEL.***)*

LURLEEN. 911! 911!

HAZEL. Don't hurt him...he's my baby!!

*(***BEATRICE, EADDY** *and* **SAM** *run out through the curtain following a screaming* **LURLEEN** *and* **HAZEL. BEATRICE** *has the fishing net and follows* **LURLEEN.***)*

EADDY. I THINK WE SHOULD PRAY!!

*(***EADDY** *begins ad lib praying. After a few wacky attempts to get the squirrel, everyone runs back through the curtain. There is another crash and a scream and then a moment of quiet with the "Jingle Bells" music still playing.* **IMOGENE** *pokes her head through the curtain and looks around, then enters and crosses to turn off the music. She is dressed as the classic Little Orphan Annie and dragging her oxygen tank.)*

IMOGENE. HELLO?

What just happened...where did everybody go? *(Beat.)* Ya know what...never mind...I don't care. It's my turn. I'm Imogene Smith, contestant number five... and I didn't miss my Magnum P.I. reruns tonight for nothing...so get ready...cause I'm doing this...*now.*

(She ad-libs as she changes the music to a karaoke track...hits play and starts to sing. *She's not a great singer and not terrible either. She really gets into her song...so much so that when a very dazed* **MARTHA** *staggers out and starts trying to twirl her baton...she doesn't notice. When* **MAUDE** *runs through screaming with Little Peanut on her face followed by* **LURLEEN** *screaming and ad-libbing...she keeps singing, unfazed until the end of her song. As* **IMOGENE** *crosses and turns off the music there is another scream and a crash as* **LURLEEN** *staggers back in disheveled with bloody scratches on her face. She is carrying a clip-in hair piece that came off during the chase. She attempts to compose herself.)*

LURLEEN. *(Delirious.)* Wasn't that wonderful? Let's have a nice round of applause for her...such a trooper. Thank you Ms. Smith.

IMOGENE. Whatever.

*(***IMOGENE*** crosses and exits through the curtain.* **LURLEEN** *calls out.)*

LURLEEN. MS. SMITH...could you please ask all the contestants to return to the stage... I am ready to announce a winner and...get the hell out of here!

IMOGENE. *(Offstage.)* WHATEVER!

LURLEEN. Normally, at this time...we would have the top three contestants come out for a question and answer... but in light of recent events...we're just gonna call this pageant done and *done.* If I could please get the

---

score sheets sometime today so that I can tabulate the scores...that would be great.

(*A* **STAGEHAND** *brings in the score sheets.* **LURLEEN** *haphazardly clips the hairpiece back onto the side of her head, then looks at the score sheets and begins adding quickly out loud.*)

LURLEEN. Nine plus seven equals sixteen...and uh... –

(**BEATRICE, EADDY, HAZEL,** *and* **MAUDE** *enter and line up wearing their evening gowns. They are all worn out.* **MAUDE** *wears her crown...and is pushing a very woozy and mumbling* **MARTHA** *in a wheelchair, still wearing her talent costume with her evening gown thrown across her.*)

BEATRICE. *Please* tell me this is almost over.

LURLEEN. This is almost over.

EADDY. Dear Lord...Thank you for this almost being over. Amen.

EVERYONE. (*Amen, Hallelujah, Etc.*)

MAUDE. Oh Hazel...that squirrel really did a number on you.

HAZEL. I just don't know what's gotten into my Little Peanut.

BEATRICE. (*Exasperated.*) OH, FOR THE LOVE OF GOD HAZEL...that was not Little Peanut you wacko...it's a wild squirrel we caught to replace Little Peanut...after Martha let him go.

HAZEL. What??? (*Beat.*) NOOOOOOOOOO...MY LITTLE PEANUT!!

MARTHA. (*Slurring.*) GUILTY! Martha's been a bad *bad* girl. Oopsie! (*Beat.*) Did I win?

(**HAZEL** *leaves her walker and grabs onto the wheelchair as* **IMOGENE** *enters wearing her gown.*)

HAZEL. I'll show you a bad girl Martha Parcell.

BEATRICE. Oh hell.

IMOGENE. What's happening?

EADDY. Hazel sweetie...I think you might want to think... before you –

MARTHA. Did I win? (*Beat.*) Where are we going? Do I get a prize?

HAZEL. Yes Martha you won...and I want to show you your *very special* prize.

IMOGENE. Uh-oh.

MARTHA. (*Delirious.*) I told you...it's *MY* year... hahhahahahaha...y'all can all SUCK AN EGG!!

(**HAZEL** *exits with* **MARTHA.**)

LURLEEN. OK...so five and eight is...uh...

BEATRICE. Thirteen...it's thirteen Lurleen!

LURLEEN. YES! GREAT!!! It looks like we have a clear winner here. So, let's get this nightmare over with... shall we? (*Bland.*) Oh yeah...you all look great...you're all winners...blah blah blah...please just come get your crap and then you can leave the stage.

(**LURLEEN** *grabs a small trophy and an envelope and steps forward.*)

Our second runner up, who will receive a trophy and a certificate for dinner for two at The Big Catch All You Can Eat Pizza and Sushi Buffet is... (*Beat.*) Ms. Eaddy Mae Clayton...yay...come get this.

EADDY. Thank you...I will cherish this forever –

(**EADDY** *crosses to get her trophy and envelope. She waves and bows, then exits.*)

LURLEEN. OK...thank you Ms. Clayton...and now to announce our first runner up...who will take the place of the winner in the event she gets pregnant...or falls and breaks a hip. First runner up will receive a trophy and another certificate for that nasty buffet...plus two tickets to the Petula Dollar Bargain Cinema. *(Beat.)...* and the winner is *(Beat.)* Ms. Beatrice Shelton.

(**LURLEEN** *crosses and gives her the trophy and envelope.* **BEATRICE** *grabs them and strikes a sexy pose.*)

BEATRICE. Who's buying me a drink boys?

(*Cat calls and whistles. She does a shimmy, wave and blows kisses as she exits.*)

LURLEEN. And that now brings us to our winner...which means, thank God...it's almost over *(Beat.)* OK...so...our new Miss Magnolia will receive all the same crap as the others...and a gift certificate from my store Belle of The Ball Evening Wear Emporium...plus the Miss Magnolia crown and sash and some flowers from Peggy's Floral Fashions...blah blah blah...and of course...the bragging rights that she *survived* this evening of total hell.

(**LURLEEN** *grabs the sash, trophy, envelopes, and flowers.*)

Ms. Maude Jenkins our current reigning Miss Magnolia will present the winner with the crown. *(Beat.)* Ms. Jenkins if you could please help me do the honors...as quickly as possible. *(Beat.)* Quickly... quickly...let's go...let's go...

(*A teary-eyed* **MAUDE** *steps forward and removes her crown. She looks at it with sadness.*)

MAUDE. Well...this is it...I'm gonna miss you little friend.

> *(She kisses the crown.)*

LURLEEN. If we could just get this over with please...thank you so much.

> **(LURLEEN** *crosses to the boom box and hits play...a light kettle drum roll, plays.)*

OK...And the winner of this year's Miss Magnolia Senior Citizen Beauty Pageant in case you haven't already figured it out...is...Ms. Imogene Smith...yay... clap y'all...or whatever –

> **(LURLEEN** *thrusts the trophy and flowers into* **IMOGENE***'s hands and tosses the sash to* **MAUDE** *and then abruptly speaks to the audience.)*

OK y'all...that concludes the train wreck...uh... pageant...thanks for coming... I'm outta' here...and if I ever say I am going to do another one of these things... please have me committed.

> **(LURLEEN** *crosses and turns off the boom box ang grabs her poster.)*

If anyone needs me... I'll be at the emergency room getting a rabies shot. *(Then.)* Never again...never... ever...*ever again* –

> **(LURLEEN** *crosses to exit then turns back.)*

NEVER AGAIN!!

> **(LURLEEN** *exits.)*

MAUDE. *(Teary.)* Well...congratulations Imogene... I hope you will wear it with pride.

(**MAUDE** *sadly places the crown on* **IMOGENE***'s head but can't let go. She grips the side of* **IMOGENE***'s head.*)

IMOGENE. *(Struggling.)* Thank you Maude... I will. OK... OK...thank you...please let go –

(**MAUDE** *steps back and turns to leave, looking back one more time before her tearful exit.*)

Well, that was certainly anticlimactic...maybe if I hurry I can at least catch the end of *Murder She Wrote.*

(**IMOGENE** *adjusts her sash and flowers and turns to exit as* **SAM** *enters. He is still wearing his Elvis attire. But carrying his Elvis wig.*)

SAM. Hey there sexy mama...lookin' good –

IMOGENE. *(Sassy.)* Oh...there you are... I was beginning to wonder if we're still married.

SAM. What are you talking about love bunny?

IMOGENE. Don't you *love bunny* me. I've barely seen you the last two days. You didn't even come out and watch me sing.

SAM. I saw a little of it while I was running around here chasing a wild squirrel.

IMOGENE. *(Glare.)* Yeah yeah...you were probably off with some two-bit floozy.

SAM. Come on sugar plum...you know you're my one and only.

IMOGENE. No, I don't...you've been running all over the place with this Clovis person and making goo-goo eyes at every woman in a three-mile radius.

SAM. *(Flirty.)* C'mon baby...you know I only have the goo-goo eyes for you sweet cheeks.

(SAM *leans in and kisses her cheek.*)

IMOGENE. *(Giggle.)* You are such a bad boy.

SAM. I'll show you a bad boy...now lay a real one on me –

> (SAM *pulls* IMOGENE *to him and gives her a smooch just as* CLOVIS *runs through and separates them.*)

CLOVIS. Hey there...gotta go...thanks for everything –

SAM. HEY CLOVIS...WAIT –

> (CLOVIS *exits quickly mumbling a pickup line.* SAM *starts to follow him.*)

IMOGENE. Sam Smith...listen to me...and listen good. It's time you paid me a little attention...don't ya think? After all, I am an official beauty queen now.

SAM. You'll always be my queen...baby doll.

> *(They kiss.)*

IMOGENE. C'mon Sam...let's go get in the back seat of the car and make out like teenagers. *(Beat.)* I'll be the prom queen and you can be the star quarterback. And we can –

> (IMOGENE *leans in and whispers.* SAM*'s eyes light up as he smiles.*)

SAM. Did you say Clovis? Clovis who?

> *(Blackout.)*

Scene Five

(The next morning in the day room. Lights up. **BEATRICE** *is lounging across the sofa wearing a colorful caftan and sipping a drink.* **EADDY** *is sitting stage left reading her Bible.)*

BEATRICE. I feel fantastic today...don't you? The birds are singing...the sky is blue –

EADDY. You're awfully chipper...are you mixing Tequila into your Slimfast again?

BEATRICE. Don't try to get on my bad side Eaddy.

EADDY. All you *have* is a bad side. *(Then.)* I haven't seen you this chipper since the last time you *(Gasp.)* Ooo... now I don't want to get into your personal business... but...did you...uh...have *relations*?

BEATRICE. Relations?

EADDY. You know what I mean *(Whisper.) Fornication* –

BEATRICE. For-nee-what?

EADDY. I'm talking about *(Whisper.)* seeeexxxx –

BEATRICE. Oh, I *know* what you meant... I just like to hear you come up with different names for getting a little pickle tickle.

EADDY. You are the *devil* Beatrice Shelton.

BEATRICE. Thank you...I try.

*(**MAUDE** enters carrying a bottle of rubbing alcohol and a cloth. She is trying to wipe off her orange-streaked tan.)*

MAUDE. Hey girls...can y'all help me?

BEATRICE. What are you doing?

MAUDE. I'm trying to get all this orange stuff off me. I look like a giant Oompa Loompa.

BEATRICE. *(Sassy.)* You said it... I didn't.

EADDY. What on earth happened to you Maude?

MAUDE. Oh, girls it was awful...there I was...out in the parking lot in that tent thing Nelda put up, to get my spray tan...wearing nothing but a plastic shower cap and my little eye goggles –

BEATRICE. WAIT...WAIT...let me picture it.

> (**BEATRICE** *closes her eyes and scowls, then laughs.*)

EADDY. *(Huff.)* Go on Maude.

MAUDE. Anyway... Nelda starts spraying me with that hose thingy...and then I hear her say "Oh crap...this is the wrong color" and she tried to turn the machine off...but she must have hit some turbo button or something... because there was this loud roaring sound and a big burst of air...and the next thing I knew, I was ass up in the petunia patch...covered in orange.

BEATRICE. Damn...I'm sorry I missed it.

EADDY. I must admit...even I would have enjoyed that.

MAUDE. Thanks girls...*thanks a lot*...first I lose my crown and now y'all are making fun of me.

BEATRICE. Oh, quit your whining Maude...you know we love you...and you don't need a crown to get attention... you're already fabulous without one...so cheer up buttercup!

> (**MAUDE***'s mouth falls open as she shares a shocked look with* **EADDY.***)*

EADDY. Who are you and what have you done with our crabby old friend?

MAUDE. Oh Beatrice...that was the nicest thing anyone has ever said to me.

BEATRICE. Of course, if you tell anyone I was nice to you, I'll suffocate you in your sleep.

EADDY. AH...there she is...our very own Miss Mary Sunshine –

> (**HAZEL** *enters with her walker. She has Little Peanut's cage.*)

HAZEL. *(Sad.)* Hey girls.

| **MAUDE.** | **EADDY.** |
| Hey sweetie. | Hello Hazel. |

EADDY. How are you feeling today Hazel?

HAZEL. How do you think I feel? My heart is broken in two. Little Peanut was my sweet baby.

MAUDE. I'm so sorry sweetie.

EADDY. I hope you're not mad at us.

MAUDE. *(Sweetly.)* If you are...you can blame Beatrice...it was her idea.

BEATRICE. Thanks JUDAS!

HAZEL. I'm not mad at y'all. I know y'all were just trying to help. But Martha Parcell is a different story

EADDY. What are you doing with Little Peanut's cage sweetie?

HAZEL. Oh girls...the most wonderful thing happened. Dee Dee over at the Vet's office called me this morning... and somebody brought in a little baby squirrel they rescued...and he needs a momma. I'm going over there right now. I'm gonna name him Little Chunky Peanut.

EADDY. Well...isn't that just precious.

(There is an announcement over the intercom.)

VOICE-OVER. "Hazel Dillard please come to the front office. Hazel Dillard to the front office. Thank you."

HAZEL. Oh, that's my taxi. I'll see y'all later.

*(**HAZEL** exits singing a happy Christmas song.)*

BEATRICE. That woman is nuttier than a squirrel turd.

*(**IMOGENE** and **SAM** enter and cross downstage center. **IMOGENE** is wearing her crown and sash. **MAUDE** sees the crown and gasps, then gingerly reaches toward it.)*

SAM. Good morning all.

EADDY. Good morning.

MAUDE. *(To crown.)* Hello little friend... I miss you.

IMOGENE. Hello Maude.

MAUDE. Not *you*...my crown.

*(**IMOGENE** rolls her eyes.)*

EADDY. Y'all are getting a late start this morning.

IMOGENE. *(Giggle.)* We were up *really late* last night.

MAUDE. I guess you were up, polishing my...uh...*your* crown.

IMOGENE. Yeah...something like that.

*(A **STAGEHAND** dressed as a mover passes through with a hand truck of boxes labeled Martha Bathroom, Martha Bedroom, Martha Fire Batons etc. The batons stick out of the top box.)*

EADDY. What's going on? Where are they taking Martha's things?

IMOGENE. Oh yeah...Martha decided to move over to Shady Oaks Assisted Living in Savannah...after that *(Giggle.)* terrible *incident* last night.

EADDY.	**BEATRICE.**
Incident?	What incident? I never hear about anything.

SAM. *(Feigning ignorance.)* Someone...and I don't know who...rolled her out in the garden last night and spread big gobs of chunky peanut butter *all* over her.

IMOGENE. When she woke up at dawn, there were a dozen squirrels feasting all over her.

EADDY.	**MAUDE.**
NO!	WHAT?

BEATRICE. *(Laughing.)* Oh, that's terrible.

MAUDE. So *that* was the blood curling scream I heard this morning.

> *(Everyone laughs but are suddenly shocked into silence as a nurse rolls* **MARTHA** *in from stage right.* **MARTHA** *is delirious, swatting at the air and muttering "Squirrel Squirrel Squirrel," Her voice escalating as she is quickly rolled off left.)*

EADDY. Bless her heart. I feel awful. *(Looking up.)* Forgive me Lord! I should have never given her that Valium.

IMOGENE. Oh no...*you* gave her Valium? How many?

EADDY. Just one...why?

IMOGENE. Because...I slipped her two!

EADDY. WHAT?

(**EADDY** *and* **IMOGENE** *are shocked and look to* **BEATRICE**.)

BEATRICE. *(Dry.)* Well shit. I guess the *four* I slipped her may have been too many.

> *(They stare at each other for a beat and then erupt in laughter.)*

SAM. Hey...has anyone seen Clovis? I went by his room, and he wasn't there.

EADDY. I didn't see him at breakfast his morning.

SAM. I haven't seen him since the pageant... I'm getting worried about him.

MAUDE. Oh...don't worry... I saw him about an hour ago... coming out of Beatrice's room.

> *(Everyone freezes and their heads turn to* **BEATRICE**.)

BEATRICE. What? Who? I have no idea what you're talking about.

> *(**CLOVIS** enters very studly. He is wearing boxer shorts, a tank top, dark socks with garters and* **BEATRICES**'s *very distinctive feather trimmed robe. He has lipstick prints all over his face. Everyone's head turns to* **CLOVIS**.)

CLOVIS. *(Deep voice.)* Hey there sexy mama...did ya miss me?

> *(Everyone's head turns back to* **BEATRICE**, *mouths agape.)*

EADDY. Wait...I don't wanna get into your personal business...but...did you...and you...uh –

MAUDE. I thought you said he was a nerd Beatrice –

IMOGENE. – and all that stuff about your reputation?

SAM. Atta-boy Clovis...I knew you could do it.

BEATRICE. OK...FINE! Not that it's anyone's business...but Clovis came over last night for a little *visit*...it had been a while for me...okay?

CLOVIS. I was hoping I'd find you babe. I'm ready for *(Air quotes.)* "round two"...if ya know what I mean.

> *(He points his "gun finger" and makes the chick chick sound and then turns to exit.)*

I'll be waiting for you...baby doll.

> *(He pops **BEATRICE** on the behind and cockily exits stage right.)*

BEATRICE. *(Giggling like a schoolgirl.)* O-o-o-o-k-a-a-a-a-y-y-y –

SAM. Well...it looks like my work here is done.

IMOGENE. Good...a "round two" sounds good to me too.

> *(**SAM** and **IMOGENE** turn to leave.)*

MAUDE. Imogene...before you go, could I just hold my...I mean...*your*...crown for old time's sake?

IMOGENE. Oh yeah...I wanted to talk to you about that Maude. I called Lurleen this morning...and was she *ever* in a hell of a mood...anyway... I told her that I really didn't care anything about this stupid pageant... I didn't want to be in it in the first place. So, I asked her if I could give the crown to someone else.

> *(**MAUDE** is shocked at the very idea.)*

MAUDE. *(Gasp.)* WHAT?

EADDY. Well, if you're giving it away... I think it should be Beatrice...right? After all...she was the first runner up.

BEATRICE. Are you kidding? I don't want it. Don't even think about it.

IMOGENE. Lurleen said she didn't give a *blankety blank* who the *blankety blank blank* that I gave it to...so... I decided to give it back to you Maude...because I know how much it means to you. So, here ya go crazy pants... it's all yours.

MAUDE. OOOOOOOOO! Thank you, thank you, thank you...and uh...if you don't mind I'll just go ahead and take the sash too!

> (**MAUDE** *snatches the sash and crown and kisses it...then puts it on her head.*)

Welcome back old friend.

> (**IMOGENE** *gives* **MAUDE** *the sash.* **MAUDE** *puts it on and begins to smile and wave.*)

BEATRICE. WAIT...wait just a *blankety blank* minute... are you saying that we all went though this ridiculous pageant...and poor Eaddy made a big ole fool out of herself for nothing?

EADDY. A fool?

> (**MAUDE** *smiles and waves as she does a step step pivot turn.*)

MAUDE. Don't be jealous Beatrice. Remember...we can't all be queen...someone has to clap as I walk by. *(She sings.)* Here she is...Miss Magnolia Senior Citizen... look at me...don't I look fine?

> (**MAUDE** *grabs flowers from a vase on the table and grandly waves as she exits.*)

BEATRICE. *(Fuming.)* I'm not sure who it's going to be... but someone has to die now.

SAM. And on that note...I think my beautiful bride and I will be off.

(*SAM takes* **IMOGENE** *into his arm, dips her, and gives her a kiss.*)

IMOGENE. Oh Sam. (*Then.*) Isn't he a hunk?

SAM.

I'M JUST A HUNKA-HUNKA BURNIN' –

(*SAM and* **IMOGENE** *exit.*)

BEATRICE. Hey...I'm going over to the YMCA. I'm gonna start a topless water aerobics class. Wanna come?

EADDY. I thought you were banned from the YMCA.

BEATRICE. They're just a bunch of old fuddy duddys...they can't stand it when I wear my hot pink thong bikini.

EADDY. Beatrice...they don't care if you wear a thong... they just asked you to stop wearing it backwards.

BEATRICE. (*Grumpy.*) Eaddy –

EADDY. (*Grumpy.*) What?

BEATRICE. You *really* need to see a doctor about getting that stick removed from your butt.

EADDY. RUDE!

BEATRICE. PRUDE!

EADDY. WITCH!

BEATRICE. BITCH!

(*They glare at each other for a second and then smile and embrace.*)

EADDY. I love you ya old Jezebel.

BEATRICE. I love you too...ya old Bible thumper.

(They turn to exit and their voices fade.)

EADDY. So...wanna enter the pageant next year?

BEATRICE. Oh yeah...sure...right after we all go ice skating in hell.

(Blackout.)

End of Play